JEZEBEL

Cassie's Ordeal

Yvette Parker

ISBN-13:9798599052432

Cover design by: Art Painter
Library of Congress Control Number: 2018675309
Printed in the United States of America

CONTENTS

PROLOGUE

There was no way Justin was going to get away with his plan. Joe was determined not to let his new money maker get away that easily. The driver pulled over at a gas station near the airport. Quickly apologizing to his passengers for the delay, he dashed inside. Joe and his thugs immediately surrounded the limo. "Get the girl now!" Joe demanded.

Terrified, Cassie quickly locked her door. One of the thugs busted her window with the butt of his gun. He dragged her out of the car by her hair kicking and screaming. Poor Justin had been choked out. He had attempted to wrestle with one of the attackers on the other side of the limo. The thugs threw her in the back of a SUV and sped off. Joe followed close behind them in his black Mercedes. Cassie knew she had to find a way out of this shit fast.

CHAPTER I: GROWING PAINS

"Cassie get your ass up! You are about to miss the bus! I'm not taking you to school!" My mother's latest boyfriend yelled. He got on my last damn nerve. I was sick of him playing Daddy. "I'm up!" I screamed back at his annoying ass. Then, I laid in my bed approximately five more minutes. I was trying to figure out what to wear. I finally dragged myself over to my closet to find my black mini- skirt and red Polo shirt. Getting dressed for school always took forever, because I wanted to look good for my boyfriend Tony.

I finished getting dressed, ate a quick bowl of cereal, grabbed my backpack, and walked to the bus stop. It seemed like an eternity before the bus got to my stop. Thoughts of my usual bus and lunchtime shenanigans helped pass the time. My mama would probably kill me. If, she knew my daily school routine.

The situation with her ex Jake would have definitely gotten me put six feet under. But that wasn't my fault.
My mother should have stopped allowing every random ass nigga she dated to live in our house. Bullshit like that was bound to happen. I started sneaking boys in the house, after the incident with Jake. Mom sent me to stay at my Auntie crib. Supposedly, her reason was that I needed more guidance. Auntie Marie was supposed to look out for me. Living there ended up being worse than living with my Mom and Jake.

The bus finally pulled up to the curb, and I pushed all that mess out of mind. Soon as I stepped on the bus, everybody started staring at me like they were crazy. I know it was because I looked good. I'm not conceited or anything. It's just that particular day, I had put more effort into my looks than usual.

I had washed my hair good last night, blown it out, and wrapped it. After I combed it out this morning, it hung silky straight down my back. Everybody at school was always asking me was it weave in my head. I can't help good hair runs in my family. My outfit was on point. I had put on my Timbs with my black knee socks that had the red stripe around the top. They accented my skirt and top nicely.

I don't know why it's so hard for people to give compliments nowadays. I held my head high and ignored the stares. I was only focused on getting to Tony's seat. He immediately stood to let me slide inside his seat. Then, the bus took off.

The bus driver never paid us any attention. A whole gang of us sat in the back drinking undetected. We disguised our alcohol in water bottles. All of us would be drunk as hell by 1st period. We took full advantage of not being under a watchful eye.

Tony was already sipping on his bottle when I sat down. "What's in there?" I asked, pointing at his bottle.

"Taste it and find out." He sarcastically responded.

I snatched the bottle out his hand. Then, took a big gulp. It was some vodka. I coughed a little bit. He laughed.

"That's what your ass gets for being so curious. Now give it back. Iesha got that weak shit y'all like to sip on." Tony stated, as he snatched the bottle out of my hand to drink more.

Iesha was sitting in front of us with Tony's homeboy Mark. I tapped her shoulder to get her attention. She passed me her drink. Then, we started chatting about girl stuff. Mark started rubbing on Iesha's titty and whispering in her ear. He acted oblivious to the fact that she and I were in the middle of a conversation. "

"Dang nigga can't you see we talking?" I rudely asked him.

"Tony check your bitch. She got her nose stuck in grown folk's business." Mark responded with an attitude.

I rolled my eyes and leaned back. I didn't feel like going back and forth with Mark that morning. I hated him. It was obvious the feeling was mutual. He was just salty because he had tried to holla at me first. I had turned him down because he wasn't my type. Then started dating Tony. Some niggas just didn't know how to take rejection.

Tony suddenly sliding his hand under my skirt, immediately took all my attention away from the drama with Mark. I glanced over at him. He just gave me this innocent look, while sliding his finger gently around my insides. I took another sip of Iesha's drink. Then, closed my eyes enjoying the feeling of my man's touch.

I really liked him and I wanted him to like me too. That's the reason I let him touch on me. Sometimes, I even licked his finger when he was done. Tony seemed to really like that. It wasn't until I got older that I understood why. Unfortunately, that lesson came from another of my mother's boyfriends too.

The bus finally arrived at school 30 minutes after I had boarded it. I stood up, straightened my skirt, and smoothed my hair. Tony stood directly behind me through the entire process. Rubbing his erection against my butt. We said our goodbyes, after we departed the bus. Then, he walked off with Mark to their 1st period.

Iesha accompanied me to our boring ass 1st period with Mr. Johnson. I used his class to catch up on sleep. I usually stayed up half the night on the phone with Tony. After my nap, I suffered through two more class periods. Finally, it was time for me to go find my boo. I always skipped most of my lunch period to meet up with him.

I walked around the gym until I found Tony in the weight room. I barged in like I was supposed to be in there. I didn't make it halfway across the room before the bullshit started. Mark began yelling, "Cassie get your ass out of here! Go where you belong!" He was such a hater. I stuck my middle finger up at him, and continued strutting over to where Tony was bench pressing weights.

I stood directly over his face for a moment.Teasing him. Then, I stepped back because I didn't want him dropping the weights on himself. He could get clumsy once he was distracted. Tony imme-diately sat up and placed the weights on the floor. Once his hands were free, he grabbed me by my waist and sat me down onto his lap. "You feel that?" he whispered in my ear. Before kissing me passionately. His full erection was poking me hard.

Mark started up his shit again, interrupting our moment. "Go get a damn room!" He hollered from across the room. Everyone else there ignored us. I wish Mark could have minded his own business like the others.

"Get up baby and follow me." Tony instructed. "

Thank God get out!" Mark said, in an annoyed tone.

I glared in his direction and stormed out behind Tony. We walked around the corner to the boys' locker room. I was always kind of nervous being alone in the locker room with Tony. Sex still made me super uncomfortable.

Don't get me wrong, it wasn't like I was a virgin. But, most of the times I had done it weren't by choice. Having sex on my own didn't feel right either. Something deep inside always made me feel bad after it was over.I would never tell Tony any of this. Because, I didn't think he would want to be my boyfriend anymore.

I just took a deep breath instead, and followed him into the back of the locker room. I attempted to mentally prepare myself as best I could for the next part. Tony pulled one of the wrestling mats from the back wall, unrolled it, and laid it down on the floor. Then he made me lay down on it.

He straddled me and started kissing me, once I laid down. Tony fingered me while we were kissing, until I got wet. Next, he spread my legs wide, moved my panties to the side, took his dick out of his basketball shorts, and slid inside me. Slowly at first. Then, he started sliding in and out of me faster and faster. The act only took a few minutes. But it seemed like forever to me. At least, it didn't hurt as bad as when Jake had done it.

Jake had threatened to get my mom to put me out. If, I didn't let him have his way with me. She was always choosing dick over me. So, I believed she actually would have put me out on the streets. Sometimes, she just acted like she hated me. Other times like she was jealous. I just didn't know what I had done to make her never once act like she loved me.

I didn't have anywhere to turn. I didn't like going to my Aunt Marie's house. Because, I didn't like the way my cousin Sean looked at me. I had seen that look in some of my mama's boyfriends' eyes. I knew what it meant. Sean finally got what he wanted from me, after mama sent me over there for sneaking those boys in the house. He didn't waste any time. The first night after my auntie went to sleep and he could hear her snoring, he came tip toeing into my room.

He held his hand over my mouth and took what I was now giving up to Tony so freely. I never told anyone what Sean did to me, because I was too embarrassed. Sean was my cousin after all. I felt my family would probably blame me. I just thought it was better to keep it to myself. My family already thought I was fast. Sean was also a little slow. They would have said it had been my idea. I didn't want to go through all that torment. So, I buried what happened in the back of my mind. Just like I had with all the others. The problem was sometimes it wouldn't stay there.

Tony was different than all the others. He really loved me. Every night we talked on the phone. All he ever really talked about was how he wanted to be with me forever. I would just close my eyes and think about the fancy life he promised every time we were in the locker room. I felt that I should have sex with him regardless of my feelings. Since, he was going to make me his wife someday. I opened my eyes, when I felt Tony nut inside me. He helped me up off the floor. Then, I cleaned myself up with a towel, kissed him while he was wiping off, and finally went to lunch.

I needed to find Iesha, because she was supposed to have gotten my lunch. While I was in the gym. I wouldn't have had time to stand in line for food, before the bell rang for next period. Luckily, she was waiting outside at the picnic tables in front of the cafeteria with my food. I didn't have to waste time searching for her.

"Girl you look a mess." Iesha said, as soon as she saw me. "Your clothes are all wrinkled up. That head is a mess. It looks like you just rolled out of bed." She slid my plate over to me. I sat down on the bench and she kept running her big mouth.

I hurried up and gobbled the food down. I didn't even respond to her. I needed to feed that alcohol, we had drank earlier on the bus. The bell rang as I was finishing eating. I rushed off leaving Iesha in mid-sentence. I didn't feel like explaining myself to my best friend again. She always told me the same shit. Cassie you're better than that. Blah blah blah. I didn't feel like hearing a lecture from her. She was letting Mark feel her up on the bus. Just because, she hadn't fucked him yet didn't make her any better than me.

Two more periods passed. Finally, it was time for me to get on the bus to go home. I was tired and slightly hungover. I just wanted to lay on Tony's shoulder and sleep all the way home. However, that wouldn't be happening this afternoon.

Tony was acting funny as hell, when I got on the bus. Usually, he just slid over so I could sit. Today however, he just sat there looking stuck on stupid. "Tony get up and let me sit down or slide over." I whined, when he didn't budge.

"No." He sternly replied, looking down at the floor.

"Come on nigga. Stop playing. This shit ain't funny. Let me sit down." I nervously replied. My heart felt like it was about to jump out my chest.Today made five or six times we had sex. I knew this nigga couldn't possibly be pulling this shit now.

"Look go sit with Iesha. I can't do this no more. You just a hoe. We all know it. Cassie, it was fun and all. But I'm done now." He loudly said.

I slapped the shit out of him. Mark started laughing. I hated his tall goofy looking ass. Iesha slid over and gave me this 'I told you so look.' I just sat down looking at the floor. I was trying my best not to cry.

Iesha walked me to the house after we got off at my stop. She tried her best to comfort me. I wasn't trying to hear nothing she was talking bout. It was all true, but right then it wasn't helping nothing. I was caught up trying to figure out why Tony was telling me were going to be together forever one minute, but calling me a hoe the next. Boys were fucking confusing. I wish I would have kept my cookie to myself.

I lied and told Iesha I was tired. So, she would go home. I needed to think without her talking my head off. I knew she only wanted the best for me. But, all I wanted at this point was to get under the covers and cry this shit out.

The house phone began to ring as soon as I walked in the door.

I picked up on the third ring. I didn't feel like talking to nobody. I hope whoever this was made this call short and sweet. "Jones residence how may I help you?" I answered the phone in the most professional way possible.

"Girl what is you sounding white for?" Tony asked.

"Nigga what do you want?" I asked, the asshole.

"Girl you know I love you. But you know how high school is. The fellas was joking on me, after you left the gym. I ain't like that shit. That's why I was acting a fool on the bus today." Tony explained.

"Nigga how you think that shit made me feel! I just gave you my body! Then, you have the fucking nerve to tell me that you don't want me in front of everybody! It was embarrassing and you made me feel like gum on the bottom of your damn shoe!" I screamed at him, all in one breath about to cry.

"Baby, I'm sorry. I didn't mean to hurt you like that. I want you. But can we keep it secret? I just don't want to hear the boys' mouth. I sure as hell don't want nobody else to have you." Tony softly responded.

"I don't know nigga. Let me think about it. I gotta go. I have stuff to do." I angrily said.

"Alright, just hit me back and let me know when you make your mind up. I love you." He calmly replied.

I responded, "I hear you." and slammed down the phone.

I walked in the kitchen and snuck some of mama's liquor. Then, went in my room to think. I did more drinking than thinking. Quickly, I drifted off to sleep. Time must have flown by. Hours later, I was awakened by my mama yelling bout some dishes in the sink. She was just getting home from work.

I hadn't even eaten yet. It wasn't my mess. Those had to be her nigga's dishes. I just pretended like I didn't hear her. Her boyfriend called her in the room. Thankfully, that shut her up. Hopefully, he would screw her to sleep so she didn't come in my room bothering me. The house got quiet again. I was still tired from drinking and the drama at school. Immediately, I fell back asleep.

An hour later I was awakened by light tapping at my window. I pulled back my curtain to see who had the audacity to be waking me up at this ungodly hour. Tony's light skin big headed ass was staring back at me, when I peered out.

"Boy, what do you want? My mama and her nigga home. You gon get me killed." I whispered.

He whispered back, "I had to see you Cass. I don't want you to leave me. I had to come talk to you face to face."

"It is the middle of the damn night! You couldn't wait until in the morning?" I questioned, sucking my teeth in frustration.

"Time waits for no man. You ain't bout to leave me girl. I had to come over here to make sure your stubborn ass wasn't trying to go nowhere." He said, tryna sound all dominant.

I rolled my eyes. "You know I love your stupid ass. I'm not going nowhere. But you gon chill on that bullshit you pulled today." I told him.

" I got you bae. We just gon chill at school and kick it after." He smoothly replied.

"Fine. You lucky I love you." I responded before closing my curtain signaling to him, I was done with the conversation.

Tony was my first love. We dated until 12th grade. I wasn't really happy about being his dirty little secret. But, I didn't want to go from nigga to nigga like my mama. So, I stuck it out. The way Tony treated me always stuck with me throughout the years. I knew there had to be a better way to be loved.

CHAPTER II: FAST MONEY

After high school, most of my friends went off to college. I didn't want to go that route. I wanted something different because, I was tired of taking classes. Besides that, I had fucked up on my SATs. My scores were low as hell. I couldn't get into college, even if I had wanted to go. I needed to make some fast money. I had to get my own place asap, because I was sick and tired of staying with mama.

Her new boyfriend loved coming to take my most precious jewel in the mornings, after she went to work. He somehow figured out how to pick the bathroom lock and would come take it, while I was in the shower. The shower kind of muffled my screams. He thought the running water kept the neighbors from hearing.

Things were for me were getting desperate, so I finally broke down and talked to my best friend Iesha about my situation. I was ashamed, but I just couldn't take it anymore. I had to get out of my mom's place by any means necessary. Iesha got me an interview with her boss at some club where she worked. She insisted it was only dancing and that the pay was fantastic. I was out of options, so I decided to go check it out against my better judgement. My audition was set up at noon. The owner wanted to see what I was working with before he let me work that night.

I took a bus to the audition. I signaled the driver to stop when the bus got near where I needed to go. My stomach was in knots, because I had never done anything like this before. Some dude brushed up against me a little too close when I was getting off, but I didn't pay it any attention. I was too busy looking down at my phone. Trying to make sure I had gotten the address correct. I figured that I probably looked like a damn fool in this little ass dress in 50-degree weather, but I had to do what I had to do. I walked the rest of the way to the club. My heels clinked on the sidewalk with every step.

I finally reached this almost run-down looking building. Why the hell would anybody want to work here? I wondered to myself. Iesha promised me the money was good. She had warned me not to judge it by the outside. . My gut was telling me to run far and fast in the opposite direction. But like I said earlier, I was desperate to change my current living conditions.

Boy was Iesha right. The inside of the place was fancy. My mouth dropped in awe as soon as I entered. It was like a club on television that the rich celebrities attended. It was decked out with leather sofas, gold poles, fully stocked bar that wrapped along the entire wall. There were mirrors everywhere too.

The owner walked up behind me while I was taking it all in. "You must be Cassie. Iesha told me that you are ready to do a lil something strange for a piece of change." He boldly said.

"Hold up I ain't say all that. I thought this was just dancing." I replied with attitude.

"Lil girl do you seriously think your friend is making 3k every night just shaking some ass." He said sarcastically. Looking me over from head to toe. I rolled my eyes. Inside I was scared as shit. This was a damn pimp. Iesha had gotten me into some bullshit and I knew it.

Fuck it I needed this fast money. Selling ass couldn't be any worse than giving it away for free. "Exactly how strange I gotta get?" I asked Joe. He had told me his name as the conversation progressed.

"Just be back here tonight. You will find out everything you need to know then. Make sure you shave and oil up. Don't nobody want no hairy or ashy bitch." Joe said. Then laughed.

"Aight nigga I hear you." I cockily responded. Then I strutted out twisting my ass confidently.

I caught the bus back home freezing the entire way. I was a mess on the inside. I couldn't believe what I had just agreed to do. Thankfully, nobody was home when I got there. I sure didn't feel like dealing wit mama or her extra friendly nigga. I had too much on my mind.

I called Iesha after I changed into warmer clothes. "Bitch why you ain't tell me u was selling ass at the club!" I yelled at her, as soon as she answered the phone. 'Girl ain't nobody selling nothing. Why you hollering in my damn ear?"

"Iesha, Joe told me you selling ass. He also told me I would have to sell it too if I work there!" I kept yelling at her.

She finally came clean after that."Look I'm going to take care of you. Just pop this magic little pill I give you later. You're gonna be so damn high you aren't going to remember the shit anyway. All the money in your hand at the end of the night will make it worth it. Just trust me ok."

Just then the front door slammed. "Cassie come here!" Mama's boyfriend yelled. "I know your yellow ass is in here."

I abruptly hung up on Iesha. I quickly stuffed some clothes in my duffle bag and jumped out my bedroom window. Fuck this. I would sleep on the streets, before I let another one of my mama's niggas touch me again. I should have ran away long ago, but I was too scared. I didn't have anywhere to go or a dime to my name. I had tried to get jobs before but they never worked out. It was always one jealous bitch that would fuck everything up.

I needed somewhere to crash until it was time to go to the club. I hit Iesha up as soon as I had put plenty of distance between me and my mom's place. "Girl why did you hang up on me?" Iesha asked, when she answered.

"That nigga Mama with now was bout to try me again. I couldn't let him do it again. I just couldn't. I hung up on you so I could get the hell out." I responded, half out of breath.

"Well look you can crash here tonight. But you can't stay until you find a place. You know I have a lot going on. Come over I'll feed you and help you get ready for tonight." Iesha said.

"Aight bet. I'm walking so its gon be a minute. I used all the money I had to go over to the club earlier." I responded back still breathing hard.

See you in a lil while I got you." Iesha said, then hung up.

Cassie understood why she could only spend one night at Iesha's. Her best friend was already over extended. That's why Cassie had kept her problems at home to herself until now. Iesha had her three kids plus her four siblings living with her. She had started popping babies out in 10th grade.

It was ironic, being she had been in my business about fucking but I had no kids. When her moms got locked up, she went to court and fought for custody of her siblings so they wouldn't go to the state. She had told me to put in for an apartment awhile ago. But somebody was getting shot out there every other night. I didn't want to live out there.

Mama's house was in the good part of the hood. Across town, where Iesha lived was ghetto as fuck. Now my ass didn't have a choice but to go. I walked with this big ass duffle bag on my shoulder weighing down my little ass arm. These damn Jordans sure wasn't made for walking far. My feet were sore like hell.

I guess it was a good thing I wasn't really dancing tonight. I sure wouldn't have been able to shake it in no heels. I finally made it to Iesha's crib an hour later. My arm felt like it was bout to fall off. I climbed the stairs to her third-floor apartment and banged on the door. It smelled like piss in the stairwell. I could hear nothing but kids screaming from behind the closed door. Iesha little sister opened the door.

"What you want?" The little girl said with her hand on her hip. She couldn't be anymore than five or six years old.

"Girl go get Iesha and learn how to talk to folks." I said to her. She yelled for Iesha. Iesha brown skin bow legged ass finally came to the door.

"Get in here before somebody snatch yo ass standing out there. You hungry? I got some spaghetti left and a little bit of tossed salad. Feeding all these damn kids I'm surprised we even have that left." Iesha offered.

"Yeah, I didn't get a chance to eat. After I hung up on you, I just dipped. I don't know how Imma do this shit tonight." I said slurping a forkful of spaghetti out the bowl Iesha had made for me. I drunk some of the Kool-Aid out the cup she had passed to me to wash it all down.

"I told you Cassie just take the magic pill. You gon feel so good you not even going to think about it." Iesha suggested.

"Iesha, I don't know bout taking no pill. I haven't done anything but smoked some weed. I couldn't even handle that high." I worriedly responded.

"Cassie put your big girl panties on. Do what you have to do. You starting on a good night. Some ballers from down south are coming to the club tonight. Cassie you are guaranteed to walk out with a couple of stacks." Iesha said to me sounding like she had been around Joe too long.

But how many of them do I gotta fuck Iesha?" I questioned.

"Joe will tell us when we get there. Like he told you earlier you will find everything out you need to know tonight at the club. What you wearing? Joe sending somebody to pick us up. He doesn't like his girls taking public transportation at night." Iesha informed me. rummaged around in my duffle bag and pulled out this little purple dress and thigh high boots to get Iesha's opinion.

"The outfit will work. Let me do your hair and makeup so you don't look so plain. I know your ass don't know to do it." Iesha said. I let her give me a makeover. She was right. I knew nothing about makeup and always wore my hair in a flat wrap.

The pill started kicking in, while Iesha was flat ironing my thick long hair. She had given me a pill and a couple of shots of liquor, before she started on my makeover. I felt like I was floating. I thought I was seeing things when I first looked at my reflection in the mirror after she was done. Iesha had me looking like a whole new person. I felt like some kind of model or something. Instead of some hoe bout to go turn tricks to keep from being homeless. I finished getting dressed, while Iesha was in the bathroom getting ready.

Iesha came into the living room looking like some video vixen. She was wearing this skin tight leopard cat suit with black thigh high boots, similar to mine. The driver called right after she was done getting ready. Iesha instructed her sister, who couldn't have been more than 14, not to bring any nappy headed boys in the house. Also, not to be smoking in the house since the baby was in there.

Then, we headed downstairs where a chromed-out black SUV awaited. Iesha got in the front passenger seat and I stumbled into the back. My head was spinning from that liquor and pill. I must have dozed off on the way to the club.

The next thing I remember, Iesha was shaking me telling me to get out because we were there. I got out and took a deep breath. Here goes nothing. I thought to myself as I made my way inside the Lion's Den.

CHAPTER III: THE LION'S DEN

I was a little unsteady on my feet. Iesha dragged me into the club by my arm. I was surprised there were actual strippers on the floor. I whispered to Iesha "I thought I didn't have to dance."

"You don't." She responded as she guided me back to Joe's office. She knocked on the door then left me there. I was scared as shit. I thought she was supposed to be looking out for me. Where the hell was she going?

I had turned to walk away but a strong arm grabbed me by the waist and pulled me through the door. "The fun is just about to begin. Where do you think you're going?" Joe looked down at me and asked.

Seated in his office was this tall muscular caramel complexion dude. He definitely had to be one of those ballers that Iesha had been talking my head off about. "Cassie this is Justin." You will be his tour guide tonight in our lovely city. I knew you were different from the other girls I have working here, when I met you. Do a good job with Justin, and you won't ever have to see the inside of any of these private rooms. Do u get what I'm saying? "Joe asked.

I was kind of embarrassed. He was basically telling me he was gon have me turning tricks in front of this fine ass dude. But pride pays no bills, and I needed to get some cash. I just mumbled, "Yeah I understand."

Justin and I left the club through a private exit. I was glad that we didn't have to walk back through that mad house of niggas and half naked chicks. There was a stretch limo waiting for us outside. The driver opened the door for us to get in. Justin started chatting me up once we were alone in the back of the limo. "My teammates arranged this. You don't have to do anything you don't want to do. I just want to go have some drinks and dinner. Whatever happens from there is totally up to you." he said.

"Look, Joe said I had to take care of you. I'm not trying to do what those other bitches are doing. So, are you sure you straight with just chilling?" I questioned him.

"Yeah, Miss lady it's cool. I just broke up with my girlfriend. The fellas were just trying to cheer me up. They said my playing sucks, because my mind is still on her and not in the game right now."

"Oh, I get it well I can definitely help you unwind. I know a place wit good music and food. Its low key so you won't have to worry about people stopping you for autographs and shit.

"Aight bet. Tell the driver the address then beautiful."

I told the driver the address. We were then whisked off. This was my first real date. It was a damn shame that the first dude to treat me like I was somebody was a client.

We talked and laughed all the way to the spot that I had suggested. Justin turned out to be really cool. He started asking a lot of personal questions. I kept switching the script back to him. I didn't want him feeling all sorry for me. We pulled up to the spot kinda quick.

The driver opened my door and Justin walked around to my side and grabbed my arm. Then we walked in. I had never been here. Some of my friends had told me about it. There was a live band playing on stage. Some chick was singing some real slow song. It had to be original, because I had never heard it before. Justin wanted to sit at the bar. I was cool wit that. He ordered us a bottle and we started taking shots. That stupid pill finally had worn off. I felt like myself again.

Justin asked me to dance. After, we had taken like five shots. I was really feeling his energy. I quickly grabbed his hand and led him to the floor. The music was still slow. He gripped me around my waist and held me close. I forgot all about this being business and just got lost in the moment. Justin was making me feel like a princess or something. He was treating me real special.

I wasn't used to being treated special. Every guy I had ever been with either wanted me to make them feel better or fuck them. They never cared about my wants or needs. I could have stayed in Justin's arms all night. But the fantasy had to end sometime. The bar had last call. We stopped dancing and drunk one last drink for the road.

Justin was tired and ready to leave. He gave me the choice of spending the night with him or getting dropped back at the club. I decided to go with him. There was no way, I was going back to the club. It's not like I had nowhere else to go. Iesha told me I could stay the night. But I really didn't have nowhere to sleep over there. She only had a two bedroom with all those kids. I thought I made the right decision. It turned out to be an unforgettable night.

The driver dropped me and Justin off at the room around three a.m. We had eaten, drank, and danced most of the night away. Justin knew my feet were killing me because I had taken my boots of in the limo. He had asked me if I wanted a piggy back ride inside. I thought he was joking, until he had stooped down and told me to get on his back.

I jumped on and wrapped my arms around him tightly, holding on for dear life. Half my ass was hanging out the bottom of my dress, but I was too drunk to care. He walked us up to the front desk to check us in. The desk clerk looked at us and just started shaking his head. He checked us in and gave us the keys. Then, we got in the elevator to go up to the penthouse.

Justin helped me off his back. I leaned up against his shoulder. "Cassie are you alright? Don't be throwing up on me now." Justin said jokingly.

"Boy I'm fine. I just need a glass of cold water and a hot shower. I'll be good as new." I responded, words slurring a bit. The elevator doors opened and Justin led the way down the hall to our suite. I staggered slightly and dropped one of my boots that I was carrying in my hand. He grabbed my arm to steady me and took over carrying my boots.

He was such a sweetheart. It was hard to believe his girlfriend had cheated on him leading to their breakup. He had told me all about their relationship while we were hanging out earlier. Justin started stripping soon as we got in the room. "Nigga what are u doing?" I asked.

"Getting out these sweaty clothes. He stripped down to his boxers then sat on the couch. "I'll wait for you to get out the shower, then I'll jump in.

I went and got in the shower. The warm water was helping me to sober up to some extent. I was still extremely tired and ready to snuggle up with Justin. If, all my assignments were like this maybe working at the Lion's Den Gentleman's Club wouldn't be as bad as I had originally thought.

" She's in the shower now. You told me this was just some new piece of pussy. She's special. It's obvious that this life isn't for her. I don't think I can do this." Justin said to the voice on the other end.

Cassie strolled in wrapped in a towel and Justin ended his call quickly. He didn't want to scare her. The night was going perfect. He was really feeling Cassie. "I'm going to wash this funk off. You don't have to wait up for me." Justin said to Cassie ,as he walked past her thick figure going into the massive bathroom to freshen up.

Cassie didn't waste any time getting into the king size bed and pulling the covers up to her neck. She was sound asleep before Justin got out the shower. He climbed in bed and wrapped his arms around her and drifted off to sleep. Right before day break, Justin was awakened by the sound of his phone vibrating uncontrollable. He quietly got out of bed as not to disturb Cassie.

When he got into the bathroom with door closed tightly, he called back the number. "What is it now nigga? I'm trying to sleep. I have to be up early to take this chick back to The Den." He whispered into the phone.

"You were supposed to unlock the door before you went in the bathroom. What the fuck happened? We sat outside the damn room almost an hour waiting on your ass. Joe said she was new , we figured you being the choir boy on the team could get her all liquored up so we could make it do what it do." Dennis, Justin's teammate, said.

"Well like I told you when you called earlier, I wasn't sure about doing this mess. I decided that I wasn't wit it. I don't care what kind of initiation bullshit y'all got going on. I thought it was gon be some hoe or something not a girl like this." Justin responded, disgusted with his teammate at this point.

"You lucky the other guys decided to leave or you would be opening that damn door. Don't think this shit over.

"Aight nigga I hear you. I'm bout to take my ass back to sleep. Fuck wat you talking bout right now."

Justin ended the call and headed back in the bedroom. Where Cassie was still sleeping peacefully. For some reason Justin felt the urge to protect her, even though he didn't really know her. Just being around her was different. She reminded him of the girls from his hometown. Instead of all these bougie bitches with fake everything, that he always seemed to be surrounded with now. She was naturally pretty, and all her curves were not surgically enhanced. He couldn't help himself. Justin pulled her closer to him and began to caress her. Starting with her soft round ass.

Cassie woke up and looked at him but she didn't say anything. Just stared into his face for a minute, before she leaned in and kissed him and wrapped her thigh around his leg. He kissed her back passionately. Then he began exploring every crevice of her body with his hands and lips. Cassie didn't know what to make of this. She wasn't used to foreplay. All the niggas that she had been with before just got straight down to the point. The two explored each other until the front desk called for them to check out.

They showered again. This time together and headed out. Once they were inside the driver asked them where they were heading. The fantasy was definitely over, because Cassie really didn't know where she wanted to go. She really didn't have any particular place to be. First, she needed to get paid. She decided back to the den and ol pimp Joe was her best bet. Before she could get out the words, Justin told the driver they were headed to the airport. He stroked her face and told her not to worry about a thing . Justin thought he could redeem himself for something he did years ago by saving Cassie.

There was no way Justin was going to get away with his plan.

Joe was determined not to let his new money maker get away that easily. The pair would soon discover. The driver pulled over at a gas station near the airport. Quickly apologizing to his passengers for the delay, he dashed inside. Joe and his thugs immediately surrounded the limo. "Get the girl now!" Joe demanded.

Terrified, Cassie quickly locked her door. One of the thugs busted her window with the butt of his gun. He dragged her out of the car by her hair kicking and screaming. Poor Justin had been choked out. He had attempted to wrestle with one of the attackers on the other side of the limo. The thugs threw her in the back of a SUV and sped off. Joe followed close behind them in his black Mercedes. Cassie knew she had to find a way out of this shit fast.

CHAPTER IV: CAPTIVE

Iesha paced back in forth through her tiny apartment talking on the phone. "I shouldn't have talked that damn girl into doing this shit. I feel terrible. Joe assured me that she would only be dancing. I knew that was a lie, when she got back from her so-called audition with him. But I still assured her everything would be fine. I really fucked up. I needed her to do this though. He told me that I could stop doing the rooms, if I could get her to come work.

I wouldn't have ever asked Cassie's naïve ass had I known this was what would happen. I was just trying to help her out and myself at the same time. I hate working there. What else am I supposed to do with all these kids. They are depending on me. I need a house. I feel like the walls are closing in on me here. The money from the club is our way out of here. I wouldn't have called you, but I didn't know who else I could let know bout this shit." Iesha finished explaining her dilemma to her cousin Donte.

Joe had been apart of Donte's life since he was eight years old. He had dated Donte's mother briefly. She couldn't deal with Joe's physical abuse and womanizing, so she ended the relationship within a year's time. Donte always blamed his mother for the breakup. She never cooked, cleaned, and was always nagging. All she wanted to do was stay high all the time.

After she died from an overdose, Donte went to live with Joe. His other family members wouldn't take him since his Mom was kind of the black sheep of the family. Joe treated Donte just like he was his biological son. He knew that Donte was kind of soft. That was a liability in Joe's line of work. So, Joe only told him so much about the daily operations of the business. Donte was a body guard and sometimes filled in as a driver. He didn't mind not knowing all the details. Being in the dark about what happened to the girls was a way to keep his conscious clear for the most part. The one thing that he did have knowledge of haunted him enough.

Donte didn't really want to get involved with the whole Cassie mess. But he was loyal to Iesha because she was the only family that he had left around there. Everybody else had either moved away or just pretended he didn't exist. Donte promised that he would help Iesha find her best friend. He knew how important Cassie was to her. He also owed Iesha big time for reasons he could never reveal to her. She would probably hate him forever if she found out. "Iesha don't worry. I got you. I'm bout to go to The Den and holla at Joe and see what I can find out." I'll hit you back as soon as I'm done talking to him. You stay there in case they drop her off at your spot." Donte hung up and grabbed his keys.

He knew Joe probably wouldn't give him any answers. But he had a good idea where to start looking for Cassie.

Iesha rolled a blunt and went on her fire escape to smoke and think, after the call. She was replaying last night in her head. She had looked all over the club for Cassie at the end of the night. Finally giving up with no success in her search, she had headed to the office to get her cut out the money for the evening. Big Ray (Joe's partner) was in the office handling the payouts. She had asked him had he seen Cassie. He wouldn't give her any information. Then she had asked about Joe. Ray responded by telling her that he didn't keep up with grown men. Luis, the driver, had come in the office and the conversation ended. Ray had instructed him to take her directly home. Iesha knew better than to argue. She was well aware of the consequences.

Cassie woke up sore as hell and slightly bruised in different clothes than the night before. Her previous night's clothes were folded neatly laying on the table next to the bed. She was oddly calm after being kidnapped. The drama of the last few days had taken their toll. She was just numb to it all at this point. She didn't feel unsafe, but she didn't feel entirely safe either.

Looking around the room, she thought to herself at least she had gotten kidnapped in style. The room had everything she needed. There was a huge flat screen that took up an entire wall, a bar cart in the corner with every brand of popular liquor, plush thick carpeting, and even one of those fancy fridges in the corner that had buttons on it that talked back to you. The room also included a sink and stove. There was a full bathroom adjacent to the room. Gazing out the windows all she could see were woods all around.

It was quiet and peaceful. She was a city girl being out in the country definitely had her out of her element.

Cassie got a bottle of water out the fully stocked fridge and settled on the couch. Watching the door waiting to be let out. There was a monitor next door to the door with a button. Seeing the two guards on either side of it, she knew getting out on her own wasn't an option. Joe soon entered with one of his flunkies behind him. "Where the fuck are we and when are you letting me out?" Cassie asked angrily before he could fully get his body through the door.

"This is my country estate only a trusted few know about it. I don't have time to be shooting niggas ova your ass. I'm a business man. This bullshit is out of my character." He said lighting up a cigar before finishing his statement.

"I'm gon keep you here until I know that fool is out of town. He is becoming a nuisance. I would put a cap in his ass, if I could. You are my new golden goose. Joe gon take real good care of you. Anything you want just press that button next to the monitor and ask. One of the staff will get it for you. Get comfortable this will be your home for a while."

Cassie couldn't believe her ears. She decided it best to be quiet and keep her opinion of her situation to herself. She wasn't a dummy and realized she had gotten herself into a world of trouble getting tangled up with Joe. She decided for now she would play his game. She would be the model captive and not give him any trouble. Looking on the bright side at least she wasn't sleeping on the streets.

Settling into Joe's was difficult at first. There was no privacy. I was only allowed out my room once a day to go outside for fresh air. I figured that this is what it must be like to be in jail. Being watched by guards 24/7. The first weeks were tough. After a while I got used to it. I wasn't being treated bad, besides being held against my will. Joe stayed true to his word and anything I asked for was given to me without hesitation.

Iesha's cousin Donte came to see me often. I was surprised Joe would let him near me. Every visit he promised that he was going to rescue me whenever the time was right. I didn't believe him. He was too stuck up Joe's ass to see straight. I didn't trust him as far as I could throw him. I believed that Joe was sending him to me just to give me false hope, so I wouldn't give him any trouble.

Despite not trusting Donte, I began looking forward to his visits. The guards acted mute. They never talked back no matter what I said to them. It was lonely being trapped with nobody to even have a decent conversation. Being kidnapped was bad, but it was still better than being at my mother's house.

Here I wasn't getting raped every time I turned around. It was kind of ironic being I was being held hostage by a pimp. I wonder if she even missed me. I imagined she was glad I was gone. Now she could fully focus on chasing nigga after nigga to put in on the bills and keep the other side of her bed warm. The longer I stayed locked up in the country the more I realized how much I hated that woman. Part of me felt like she knew what those niggas were doing to me.

She was just too scared of being alone again and having no financial assistance that she offered me up like a buffet to their trifling asses.

I think that's why my daddy left and never came back. He sensed the evil in her and didn't want it rubbing off on him. I think besides trying to get over being molested, I just wanted somebody to love me like Daddy did. That's why I was sleeping around before I got myself into this mess. Being locked in here I had entirely too much time to think.

Donte suddenly appearing brightening my thoughts. "Come on lets go." He said, as soon as he walked through the door. I jumped up and rushed out the door with him. Excitedly thinking Joe was finally setting me free. However, I just ended up accompanying him on a walk along one of the trails in the woods next to the property. I guess it was better than nothing. I had already been outside for the day. If he hadn't visited, then I would have been locked inside until the following day.

Donte was usually cracking jokes and very talkative, but today he was kind of quiet. "Boy what's wrong with you?" I finally asked him. I couldn't take his funny acting shit no more.

"Something happened to Iesha. She got hold of some bad shit. We not sure if she gon pull through or not." My whole world seemed to stop after he said that. Iesha was really the only person that I had left in the world. I had to get out of here to see her. Joe was due to come later. Maybe, I could talk him into letting me go see Iesha.

I sat with Dontae on the dock by the lake. After our walk along the trail. I could feel eyes watching us the entire time. No doubt we were being watched by the rest of Joe's little squad. I didn't mind being under surveillance so much with him there. Somebody treating you like a human being, instead of property went a long way. "Donte do you ever want to do something different? I know when you were a little boy your dream wasn't to work for Pinkie."

He burst out laughing at my statement. "Girl you ain't got no sense. Joe's suits look way better than that nigga on Friday."

I retorted back giggling, "Hell all he missing is the juice curl dripping everywhere. They would be twinning then.

Donte got all serious responding, "On some real shit Cassie, I never even thought about the future after my moms died. I just felt like life was over. I just starting living life going through the motions. Just trying to make it from one day to the next. She wasn't much of a Mom, but besides Iesha that's all the family I really had in the world. If Joe hadn't took me in, I don't know what I would have ended up doing.

"Something other than being a coochie protector I'm sure." I responded, rolling my eyes disgusted with how far up Joe's ass he was really stuck. "Donte your ass betta take care of my best friend. You know we all we got and I can't do shit stuck in here." I said glancing at his face for a reaction.

"Well, nobody told your red ass to run. What the hell you thought this shit was Cas. This here ain't no game. Most of the time ain't but one way out and that's in a body bag. Nobody can't even buy your way out. The dude you ran away with brought his ass in the club after Joe almost killed him, trying to buy your way out of trouble. He offered Joe's ass half a mil. Joe turned it down without batting an eye.

He did counter his offer with 20 mil, but that was just to consider letting you go. You're highly requested. Joe doesn't know, but I did some digging on his computer before I came out here looking for you. He has this site on the black web. Those dudes overseas having a bidding war on your head. He's trying to sell you off to one of those Chinese businessmen. Joe is involved in a whole sex trafficking ring."

I thought about all the information Donte had just laid in my lap. Finally, I replied, "That's why he ain't made me fuck on nobody since I been staying out here. He is just biding his time. Waiting, so he can ship me off for his big payday. Getting off topic I asked him, "How you gon let Iesha get tangled up in all this shit? You're her big cousin. Almost like a brother to her. You were supposed to look out for her."

Donte looked away for a long time before he answered, "Well you know my ma was dead, and Iesha's mom got locked up. I don't make enough to take care of all of them. I tried to talk to Joe for help, but he said that he wasn't running a daycare center. Iesha went down to The Den and talked to him, after I let her know what he had said. Joe put her on and here we are."

I looked at him and rolled my eyes. "Nigga that's your baby cousin. I still don't understand how you could live with that. I know there had to have been another way. If I had known I would have talked her out that bs."

Donte stood over me looking down at my face a moment before he spoke. "Well, ain't you the pot calling the kettle black. Hush girl and let me walk you back to the house. I'm tired of being watched by all these damn guards. I'll tell Iesha you good and that you asked about her. Behave yourself. Maybe Joe won't ship your ass off to China."

I replied back, more confident than I was actually feeling "I'm not worried about that shit. I'll be back in the city before you know it. Joe is just trying to teach me a lesson that's all."

He sarcastically replied, "Ok Billy bad ass. You think that. I'll be back in a few days or so."

We were back at my prison as I so lovingly called the house by the time, we finished our chat. I reluctantly walked in my room. Being outside for so long had felt good. The conversation with Donte was weighing heavily on my mind. I was way more concerned than I had let on to him. I had to get out of there somehow.

There wasn't anything I could do about my predicament at that exact moment. I needed energy to come up with a plan. I pressed the button next to the monitor and ordered my dinner. I switched on the tv to try to distract myself from the mess I was in. Skimming through the channels I saw my face.

I stopped immediately stunned by who the anchor was interviewing. My mama was on tv, holding a picture of me telling the news anchor about my abduction and the reward. She looked really bad. Tears were spilling from her eyes.

Justin hadn't given up on me. Instead of taking Joe's no, he had decided to offer a two-million-dollar reward to anyone that found me There was a nationwide manhunt for me now. I was shocked. I couldn't believe my mom actually stopped chasing dick long enough to find me. Maybe she did love me after all.

I figured Justin had gone back to his life. This man I hardly even knew was going through all this trouble for me. No man had ever done that for me. I was overwhelmed with emotions. After my least favorite guard brought my food. I went to sleep. I needed to regroup for whatever was next. One thing I did know was that tomorrow was finally looking brighter.

◆ ◆ ◆

Joe was sitting at his desk in his office counting money. The tv was on for background noise. Nobody was there yet, and he hated the silence in the club before opening hours. The interview with Cassie's mom caught his attention. He dropped the stack of bills that he was about to put in the counting machine.

Fumbled around on his desk for the remote and turned the tv up. His mouth dropped open, when his name was mentioned. Everything he had been working on for years was ruined. Justin had one job and he couldn't even do that. Nobody told him to fall in love with the bitch. Joe couldn't believe Justin sold him. She was rare, but still it was the principal.

Joe needed fresh young meet for his overseas clients. They didn't really care for the older women.

He asked Donte if he had any young female friends in need of fast cash. He initially told him no. After Iesha's Mom went to jail, Donte told him about her. Joe told him exactly what to say to her to make her come down to the club and he did.

Donte had felt bad for deceiving his cousin. Joe had assured him that it was in her best interest. Back then Donte was young and naïve. Once Joe saw how attached Donte was to Iesha, he changed his mind about trafficking her. He decided to put her to work in the private rooms instead.

One day Iesha was waiting for him to pay her at the end of her shift. Cassie had video called her while she was waiting for him to count all her money out. Joe took longer than necessary so that he could get a look at the voice on the other end of her line. He knew Cassie was the one he had been searching for as soon as he laid eyes on her. She was the exact description that his clients had been requesting. He hurriedly put her up for auction as soon as he had talked Iesha into sending him a picture of her. He devised a plan to get Cassie into is clutches.

He brought her name up to Iesha constantly. Finally, he gave Iesha an offer she couldn't refuse. He offered her more money and a new position in the club. He knew she was tired of fucking and sucking in the private rooms every night. A few months later, Iesha delivered Cassie just as she had promised. Bids were in the millions for Cassie by then. None of that mattered now. Joe was about to lose the club he spent years developing into a money-making machine, his freedom, and his golden goose.

Donte was at the hospital checking on Iesha. He felt terrible that his cousin was laying in a hospital bed and it was partly his fault. Joe had given him some pills and weed to give to Iesha. He had said that it was a thank you for getting Cassie to the club. Donte had given her the package when he had dropped her off after work. A few hours later he was getting a call that she was in the hospital and to come quick.

The guilt had been eating at him ever since. His phone rang startling him because he was deep in thought. "Look I need you to come pick me up immediately from the den and take me out to the country. I've already called my pilot to meet me there. I've got to make sure Cassie is securely transported and get out of town myself." Joe hurriedly instructed then hung up. He didn't give Donte any time to respond.

The news caught Donte's attention as he was heading out the door. He stood in front of the television and watched the interview with Cassie's mother and a plan began to form in his head.

Donte made a few calls. Then went to pick Joe up from The Lion's Den. They were stopped at a traffic light down the street from the club as a line of police cards sped past. Donte was glad he was on his own car and not one of Joe's SUVs. They would have surely been spotted. Joe ducked down in the passenger seat until the police cars had passed. Then sat up and wiped his brow with relief. He and Donte gave each other a relieved look. "That was too damn close for my comfort. I'm not trying to get locked up behind your ass." Donte said to Joe.

"Neither of us are getting locked up. After I make sure Cassie is off to China, you're going to take me to a little friend. I need a whole new identity before I get out of here. It should only take a few minutes. I called him right after I called you" Joe said.

"Well why didn't we do that first?" Donte questioned. "Because making sure Cassie isn't found is most important. I would lose millions if they find her." Joe explained.

"But what about your freedom nigga?" Donte asked thinking Joe's whole idea was stupid.

"What did you just say to me?" Joe asked.

"Nothing." Donte responded and turned the music up loudly. He was just glad that this nightmare with Joe was almost over. They rode in silence listening to the music the rest of the way to Joe's country estate where he was holding Cassie.

They pulled up to the estate which was eerily dark. The guards weren't at their usual post. "Where the hell is everyone?" Joe asked Donte.

"How the hell am I supposed to know?' Donte quickly responded back.

"Go look for the girl. I'm about to make some calls." Joe instructed. Donte already had one leg out the car before Joe could finish his sentence. Joe was really scared. He had never been without any protection. When the lights came on and he saw his guards posted back in their spots, he got more comfortable. Must have been an outage or something he thought to himself.

Donte went in to get Cassie. They didn't have much time so he hoped she would move fast. When he appeared at her door, she was surprised to say the least. "What are you doing here?" she asked.

"Didn't I tell you that I would rescue you. I aim to do just that. Just trust me ok. Now come on. We have to go now." He grabbed her hand and began to lead her down the completely empty hallway. Cassie noticed all the guards were gone, but she didn't ask any questions. Freedom was close that's what was important. Suddenly a whirring of a helicopter could be heard overhead. Donte rushed her out the building and onto the plane. Justin grabbed her hand, helped her settle in, and they took flight.

Joe watched the helicopter take Cassie away. He smiled thinking that he had won. Donte looked at his phone and checked his deposits. Sure enough two million had hit his account. He gave a loud whistle. The guards that had positioned themselves near the car earlier in the darkness, popped out and began to rain gunfire down on the car where Joe sat.

The car was surrounded on all sides. Joe never had a chance of making it out. The plan had been risky. But Donte knew after he saw the news report it was only of matter of time before everything fell apart. He called Justin immediately. He had given Donte his number the night he went into the club trying to buy Cassie back. After Justin assured him that he would be paid, Donte called one of the guards he knew. They coordinated the attack, and he promised them a cut out of the two million.

He would have gotten Cassie out way before now for free, but he didn't have the means to do so. Joe getting killed wasn't only to save Donte's life (Joe would have killed him for double crossing him) but all the other ones that he was ruining as well. Tonight, wouldn't make up for all the wrongs Donte had ignored but it would make his nights a lot less restless.

Cassie burst into tears when her eyes adjusted to the darkness and she realized that Justin was the man helping her in the plane. He wrapped his arms around her. "It's over now. Only good things ahead." He assured her while stroking her hair.

"How did u do all this?" she asked bewildered by everything that had just happened.

"Basically, money talks and bullshit walks. I didn't care if I had to spend every last dime, I was going to get you back. Just rest. We will be landing in Maldives soon. After what you have been through, you deserve to be pampered. I'm taking you as far away from the madness as possible to do just that." Justin said, in a determined tone.

Cassie had more questions but she just let them go. She was finally free after months of captivity that's all that mattered right now. She closed her eyes, grateful for this new chapter that was about to begin in her life. But, in life things are often not as they seem and she was about to experience that first hand.

CHAPTER V: ILLUSIONS

Donte arrived at the hospital around noon. He still hadn't told Iesha that her best friend was gone. Neither had he told her about Joe. Life for Iesha was about to change drastically. Unsure how all this instant change would affect his baby cousin, he trudged down the hall. Lost in his thoughts not paying attention to where he was going, he plowed head first into a nurse. "I'm so sorry miss." He hurriedly apologized. She looked up at him and smirked. When he got to Iesha's room she was already dressed and ready to go." What took your ass so long? I'm ready to get the hell out of here" Iesha rudely asked Donte.

"First of all, who you talking to like that. You lucky I came and picked your nappy head up." Iesha had walked up to him and wrapped her arms around him before he finished talking shit. Donte patted her on the back, while holding her in a tight hug. He let her cry her weeks of frustration out on his shoulder. Iesha had been through hell and back trying to recover.

"You want me to push you out in the wheelchair girl?"

"No nigga I can walk. Just carry my stuff" Iesha replied. Donte grabbed her overnight bag. Then all the flower arrangements and care packages Cassie had sent. They made their way outside. Donte placed all Iesha's stuff in the trunk When they reached his new truck, he got in the driver's seat and unlocked Iesha's door. Once he was satisfied, she was securely settled into the truck he sped off towards Iesha's new home. "Donte where the hell are we going?" Iesha asked a few minutes into the ride. She had noticed that they were not going in the direction of her apartment."

"Hush, sit back, and enjoy the ride. What the hell else do you have to do?" Donte replied. Iesha glared at him, folded her arms, and then turned her head to look out the window. The city skyline faded away to countryside.

Finally, they pulled up to the gate in front of the house. Donte punched in a code, the gate opened, and they continued driving up to this enormous two-story brick house. There were a few buildings in the backyard that matched the brick of the main house. A matching truck almost identical to Donte's sat in front of the house with a big red bow. Movers were already there unloading all this expensive looking furniture when they pulled in. "Donte I'm not helping move no damn furniture" Iesha whined.

"Girl you don't have to move any furniture this your shit. They moving it in for you" he responded. She looked at him bewildered.

"What the hell did you do Donte?" Iesha asked skeptical that she really owned everything.

"It ain't even like that. I owe you more that you know." Donte said. Not really answering her question. He still wasn't ready to tell his baby cousin everything. There would be plenty of time for that. Right now, he just wanted her to enjoy the moment. He handed her an envelope without saying a word.

It contained more money than Iesha had ever had in her possession all at once. It was enough for her to take care of her family for a long time without having to worry about anything. She just started crying at a loss for words.

The plane landed in what could only be described as paradise. It was so beautiful. The water was turquoise my favorite color. The sand on the beach was the whitest I had ever seen in my life. Justin had booked us a bungalow on a private island. We were taken there by a speedboat after we departed the plane. The only people on the island were Justin & I, a chef, and maid. Justin said that I wouldn't have to lift a finger the entire time we were on vacation. We stayed there a week. It was a life changing experience for me because I had never been out of my city let alone the United States.

Our last night on the island Justin took me for a walk on the beach. I just got overwhelmed with emotion and began crying like a baby out of nowhere. We were walking hand and hand in silence and he just randomly asked me if was I ok. Then the flood gates just opened up.

"I don't know. All of this feels like a fairytale. I feel like my knight in shining armor has come along and rescued me. But fairytales ain't real. Women like me don't get happy endings. I appreciate you letting me get my head together. But what do you want? I just don't understand why you would pay all this money and go through all this trouble for a girl you only met once."

"Let's have dinner love and I'll explain." Justin said, as we approached this nice dinner set up on the beach. Justin had gone all out. There were musicians playing music, candlelight, and a buffet of food placed on a fancy decorated table. There were two thrones as our seats. Who puts thrones in the middle of the beach? I guess this nigga. So, I guess Queen Cassie I was for the evening.

Justin spoke again after they were seated and had begun eating. "Cassie, since the moment I saw you I knew all that I wanted to do was protect you. I don't know the whole story about how you ended up in this mess with Joe, and I don't care. All I know is he is gone now. I'll do anything to keep you safe from this day forward. There's some things you need to know, but now isn't the time."

Cassie was tired of drama so she didn't push the subject any further. The next thing she knew Justin was down on one knee with a ring asking her to be his wife. This was all surreal. She looked Justin in his big brown eyes and quickly answered his proposal with a yes. At this point it was all about survival, and Justin seemed to be her best bet. What could it hurt to stay with him until she could figure out her next move. She pushed all the doubts out of her mind and enjoyed her last night in paradise with her new fiancé. Perhaps, she should have listened to her intuition because trouble was brewing on the horizon.

Iesha directed the movers on where to place her new furniture. Her family came bursting through the door interrupting her decorating. Donte had gone to pick them up, after he had dropped her at the house. He wanted to surprise her, so he didn't tell her what he was going to do when they were together earlier. Iesha greeted her children first. She hadn't seen them in a month. She was beyond overjoyed to be reunited with them again. After showering them with hugs and kisses, she got around to everyone else. Donte slipped out unnoticed during the reunion. Iesha ordered everyone off to pick out a room and start unpacking. Things were finally looking up for her and she couldn't be happier.

Donte left Iesha's and headed out to Joe's country property. He needed to clear his head and it was serene out there. The last few weeks had been a blur. He needed time to think and plot his next move. He had more money than he had ever had before. It was overwhelming.

The next thing he wanted to do was get Iesha's mom released from jail. Donte felt that the debt he owed his cousin would be paid in full once her mom was free. He had found out years ago that his Aunt had gotten locked up for drug charges that she had taken for Joe. He didn't have the heart to tell his cousin.

His mom had overdosed, when she found out Joe had cheated on her with her sister. Donte being young had sided with Joe, because he knew what kind of woman his mother had been. Now that he was older, he did wonder how his life would have turned out if he had taken a different path. When Cassie had asked him about all this, he didn't want to reveal his true feelings to her. Donte didn't like being vulnerable with anyone.

He finally reached the estate. It looked welcoming without the guards surrounding it as they had been for months while Cassie was there. Donte decided to go sit on the dock that Cassie and he had shared their last afternoon together, before he had rescued her. He came up with a plan to get his Aunt out of jail. He decided he would go to Joe's old house and dig through his things, and see if he could find any influential people that Joe had been connected to. Donte was sure in Joe's line of work there had to be someone that Joe had in his pocket. When he found that person, he would pay them off to set his Aunt free. After Iesha's mom was free, he would move away and start a new life.

Donte felt better. He was glad he had decided to make the drive out there. Joe crept into his thoughts. He kind of wanted to give him a proper burial. Despite all the things that he had done, Joe was the only father figure Donte ever knew. He still had love for him and he couldn't deny that. Donte stood on the dock and said his goodbyes to Joe, so that he could finally have peace. Then, he got into his truck to set out to execute his plan. That drive seemed like the longest one in history.

The morning after the proposal the couple flew back to The States. They went straight to Justin's mansion right outside of ATL. Cassie had always lived up North, being down South was like a culture shock. She didn't understand why her fiancé wanted to live out in the boondocks. Cassie missed her best friend terribly, but she wasn't sure if she should contact her yet because of everything that had gone down.

Justin took her out on the town nightly to try to keep her mind off of the past. He had quit the team and started working at his father's law firm. He didn't want to travel so he could be at home with his future wife. Justin also wanted to distance himself from the guys that were still upset with him, because he didn't go along with the original plan for Cassie.

Cassie settled into her new life effortlessly. It was definitely a big change of pace for her. She was reflecting over the difference in her life as she loaded the dishwasher. Doing dishes was something that she usually didn't do, because Justin didn't like her doing housework. They had maids to handle that sort of thing. Cassie still like to do it from time to time because she didn't want to get caught up in this new wealthy lifestyle. She wanted to remain humble.

Volunteering at the shelter was another way she gave back and helped her to stay grounded. Justin came in and hugged her from behind and kissed her cheek as she was loading the dishwasher. Teasingly Cassie said, "Lewis you know my husband is a jealous man. He would fire you in a second if he knew you were making moves on his future wife."

Justin humorously replied, "I know damn well that 60-year-old butler isn't making moves on my woman." Then, he smacked his fiancé on the ass. They both laughed.

"Hell, I doubt he remembers the moves to make." Cassie said. Justin chuckled again.

"We are going out tonight. I have been so busy the last two weeks we haven't had a chance to just go out and just kick it. Those business parties you accompanied me to don't count." Justin explained.

"Where are we going? I need to know so I can figure out what to wear" Cassie whined to him.

"Just put on something casual. We are just going out for drinks and to grab a bite to eat. Don't take all night getting ready you know how you do" Justin grumbled.

"Hush I'm bout to go get dressed now. Are you wearing that suit or changing into street clothes? Cassie questioned.

"I'm changing now woman. I don't have to wear this mess when I'm not at work." Cassie gave him a quick kiss.

An hour later the two were dressed and ready to head out on the town. Justin wore a pair of distressed denim jeans, a black sweater and his Gucci sneakers. His platinum Rolex adorned his wrist. The platinum chain he had around his neck accented his watch nicely. Cassie's outfit complimented his. She donned a black mid-thigh length form fitting black sweater dress and a pair of thigh length black leather boots. Her jewelry was simple. She just wore her five-carat diamond engagement ring and sparkling three carat diamond hoop earrings. She had her box braids half up in a bun and the other half flowing down her back.

Justin held his future bride's arm and escorted her out the

house to his chromed out black Mercedes SUV. He opened the passenger side door and closed it firmly after Cassie had gotten settled inside. Not before slapping her on the ass before she was fully seated. "Woman you're not wearing any panties." Justin exclaimed after feeling nothing but flesh underneath his hands.

She looked at him and smirked, "Mr. Milton I have no idea what you're talking about."

"Mmmhmm keep playing with me woman. We aren't going to make it out the driveway if you keep this up." Justin seductively whispered. He stopped lusting over his woman long enough to actually get in the vehicle and drive them to dinner.

Justin pulled up to The Spot this local restaurant that his best friend owned. It was known for strong drinks and the best food ATL had to offer. Dinner was definitely not Justin's motive for frequenting the establishment that evening. Cassie and Justin bypassed the long line of patrons waiting to enter. The hostess immediately led them to a two-person table because more people would be joining them shortly. Iesha looked at him puzzled. "Justin what other people coming?"

"Don't worry your pretty little head about it. Just order a drink until our guest arrive." He mysteriously responded. Cassie ordered Crown with Coke. Justin ordered Henny on the rocks. They sat and sipped in silence for a few moments. "Oh, they're here now." Justin said, after he glanced up from his drink to look at the door.

Cassie almost gulped half of hers down in one swallow after she saw who had entered. It was like seeing a ghost. She jumped up and raced to embrace Iesha tightly before she could even make it all the way to the table. "Bitch what are you doing here!" Cassie exclaimed in excitement. Her excitement immediately dwindled a little bit when she saw Donte strolling in after her. She had a lot of questions for that nigga.

She planned to have answers for them all by the time she left that night. Cassie sat back down, finished her drink, and summoned the waiter over for another. Iesha sat down looking rather uncomfortable and ordered a Dr. Pepper. Donte walked over slowly to join them. Looking like he was being led to an execution.

"Well, the gangs all here let's start this shall we" Justin said a little too happily. Cassie looked around bewildered.

"Start what exactly?" she timidly asked.

"Baby I can't get married to you without you knowing the truth. The whole truth. I have seen how the past has been haunting you over the last few months. I want you to know you don't owe these niggas shit." Justin said, slamming his glass down on the table. Donte looked at him with a icy stare.

"Iesha, what the hell is he talking about?" Cassie nervously asked her best friend.

"Go ahead and tell her. I didn't pay y'all to come all this way to just sit here and look crazy." Justin coaxed.

"We ain't ask you to do that. We have our own money. The only reason that we are here is because we feel like we owe Cassie the truth" Iesha angrily responded.

"Well get to talking." Justin demanded, lifting his shirt just a bit so they could see the revolver in the holster on his side. What in the entire hell Cassie thought to herself. She had never seen Justin act like this. He was one of the gentlest men that she had ever known, so she thought. She had no idea he owned a gun.

Donte took a deep breath. "I guess I'll start. You ending up in the Lion's Den wasn't an accident. Joe had been planning it for months." Cassie's mouth dropped open and Donte continued. "Joe talked me into getting Iesha to work for him. Then he used her to get to you." Cassie looked at Iesha in disgust.

"Cassie, I didn't know what he was planning. He just kept bugging me to get you to come down there, after you had video called me that day at work. I didn't think it would hurt nothing. He promised me I could stop turning tricks and that he would pay me more. I needed the extra money. I was tired of tricking every night. This was my way to a better life so I took it."

"Where is the bastard now?" Cassie asked distraught. They all replied in unison, "Dead."

Justin took over the storytelling. "I paid Donte off to save you. The reward money that I was offering I gave to him. He made an arrangement with Joe's goons to get you out. Joe's body is in the bottom of the lake out where you were being held." Donte was shocked by Justin's revelation. Justin continued. "Joe had to die. None of us would have ever been safe if we let him live. All the men out there weren't Joe's. Some of them were mine. After they were sure Joe was dead, they massacred his goons. As of now, The Lion's Den never existed.

My father is a very important man with a lot of connections. He helped me clean this mess up. We can all move on from this bullshit like it never happened. Cassie I'm not perfect by a long shot, but I need you to fully trust me if you're going to be my wife. Now that you have an idea of the person, I truly am I'll leave that up to you to decide. These people betrayed you to the fullest. If you want to savage your friendship, that's on you". Cassie took another big gulp of her drink. It was a lot to process.

It was obvious why Justin wanted to meet in a public place who knows what would have happened if they had met in private. They all were waiting for Cassie to respond. "Just take me home." she said glaring at Justin as she stormed out leaving everyone at the table speechless. Good thing she had snuck that blunt from one of the maids earlier.

She had been smoking on the low lately. Her anxiety was at an all-time high. She was afraid if she made a wrong move Justin would send her packing. They barely knew each other. She still didn't fully understand why he wanted to put on a cape and be captain save a hoe. She leaned against the truck smoking, waiting for Justin to come out and take her home. All of sudden, she heard gunshots rang out. Justin came running out the restaurant. He yelled at her to get in as he unlocked the door and they screeched off into the night.

"What did you do?" She screamed at him.

"Don't worry about it. The less you know the better. Just know we good. Nobody is saying shit, this my city."

So overwhelmed with emotions, she burst out crying. Who

was this gun carrying gangster next to her. She thought to herself. Justin flew down the highway going in the complete opposite direction of their home, alarming Cassie.

"Where you taking me nigga?" She worriedly asked.

"We need to get away. I just bodied two people in the middle of a crowded restaurant. I know nobody is going to say nothing. But it's always better to be safe than sorry." Justin calmly responded.

"You killed them!" Cassie screeched sobbing uncontrollably.

"That nigga Donte wants you bad. I can tell how he looks at you. After everything I went through to get you, I'm not letting anyone take you away. Iesha the reason you almost got shipped overseas to be a sex slave. Anybody that hurts my baby gotta go." He peeked at Cassie out of the corner of his eye. He could tell by the look on her face his insane plan had worked. He was quite proud of himself. Now he had Cassie all to himself, forever if he had it his way.

This nigga crazy crazy Cassie was thinking. She knew she would have to thug this shit out with Justin for minute. Cassie had never felt so alone in her life. For some strange reason of all people, she started thinking about her mama. She hadn't thought about her in months.

Deloris had started drinking on the bus ride home. She had been finding comfort in the arms of Jack, in the evenings after work. She had always been a drinker, but ever since her baby girl's memorial service it had gotten much worse. If it was a good night, she would at least mix the liquor with some coca cola.

After months of not finding Cassie, everyone just assumed she was dead. Her case was closed and Deloris was left with nothing but guilt. It had been easier for Deloris to convince herself that it was Cassie's fault for being so young and pretty, than to take accountability for the type of men she was allowing in her home.

What man wouldn't be tempted with a teenage girl prancing through the house in miniskirts, crop tops, etc. She had grown jealous of the looks that she always caught the men she brought home giving her daughter, when they didn't think she was looking. Deloris still looked good for her age, but her butt wasn't as firm as it used to be and her titties had begun to sag.

She had turned a blind eye to the sexual abuse to have another warm body in her bed at night, and somebody to go half on her bills. Living on the good side of town wasn't cheap. If she had to offer her daughter up now and then to keep her lifestyle, then that's just what it had to be.

Now with Cassie gone the guilt was eating away at her mother's insides, and she just couldn't take it anymore. Jack mixed with guilt would be the motivation for her actions that particular evening. She walked into her home and just sat down at the table. Deloris took another gulp of her liquor, then she yelled for her latest boyfriend Mike. He had been the one that made Cassie run away.

Tonight, Deloris decided she would do what she should have a long time ago. When Mike walked in the kitchen, Deloris slid her 22 pistol out of her purse and shot him in the chest. His body dropped instantly, before he could utter a single word. She stood over him. Looked down and spit on him, as she watched the life leave his body. Then, she kicked him and took her seat back at the table and had another drink.

Deloris begun talking to herself out loud, "This was for you baby girl. I hope you can forgive your mother for making you leave through this bullshit. I should have sent you off to live with your Daddy. I was too mad at him for leaving, so I kept you away from him. I was a terrible mother. I failed you in every way.

I hope you are looking down at me now, and you see how much you really did mean to me. I love you fly high baby girl." Those were the last words Deloris would ever say. She had decided she was tired of living with the pain.

Justin had introduced me to a lot of people, since we had gotten back from being on the run as he called it. I had two circles of friends. Olivia and her clique, which were bougie as hell. I got introduced to them at some function his parents were having. He told me that it was important for me to hang out with influential women. I went to their boring ass brunches and dinner parties. I hated being around them, it was draining having to try to be perfect all the time.

My other circle of friends was Tangy and her crew. Justin couldn't stand me hanging out with Tangy, even though it was his cousin. She had rescued me from Olivia, the night of his father's party and we had been tight every since. She worked for his father. Justin said he didn't know why his father gave her ghetto ass a job.

I had snuck over to Tangy's a few hours after Justin went to work. She had invited me over for a spades game and drinks. I loved kicking it at her crib, because I could just be myself. Tangy had invited a couple of her guy friends over in addition to the usual female crew.

One of them was fine as hell. He had been around a couple times before. If I didn't know that Justin was half crazy, I probably would have tried him. After me and my partner lost our game, I stepped outside on the porch to smoke a blunt and try to sober up a little bit before the drive home. We had been downing shots, and I was starting to feel them all at once. Weed helped me to balance the alcohol.

Tyrie walked outside a few seconds later, lit up his Newport, and started chatting. "Miss lady don't run off. We looking forward to beating your ass again on that table."

I looked over at his sexy ass and laughed. "We just gave y'all that win. We coming back strong next game."

"You sure?" he chuckled, pointing at my partner slumped on the couch. That bitch was dead to the world. The Henny had knocked her into a deep sleep.

"I guess I'll be heading home. My man will be home soon." I said.

"Oh, you got a curfew miss lady. Ok I feel that." Tyrie ridiculed."

"It's a respect thing. That's all. You wouldn't know anything about that" I defensively explained."

"Alright Aretha get on home now." he sarcastically responded. I decided to ignore his last comment. I went back into Tangy's place, grabbed my sweater off the couch, and walked out to my Charger. Screeching out the driveway, I sped home.

Justin would be mad as hell if discovered I was out in the hood again. I did not feel like dealing with his attitude or hearing his mouth. He had flipped the last time, he found out I was over there. He had been acting pretty normal since the restaurant incident besides that. After seeing that touch of crazy, I wasn't playing with him.

I never wanted to see that side of him again, if I could help it. I raced into our driveway noticing Justin just pulling into our garage. Shit. Now I had to come up with some excuse as to where I been. I parked beside him and got out my car nonchalantly.

"Hi baby." I greeted him as I gave him a hug and kiss. Justin kissed me back passionately, grabbed my hand, and led me lovingly into the house. He didn't even ask about my whereabouts. Which was a shocking. He usually wanted to account for me every minute of the day. Whatever was going on with him today I liked it.

The house smelled great. Clara already had dinner prepared. I was lucky she just assumed what time we would be home. Justin and I washed up and sat down for dinner and chit chatted throughout. I still had thoughts of Tyrie dancing around in my head all through the meal. He was so damn fine. I knew I should have been happy with Justin's crazy ass.

He gave me everything I could ever want or need. No other man had ever treated me as good as he did. But something was just missing between us. I couldn't quite put my finger on it. I finished the last of dinner up and went out to smoke. It had been a long day and I needed to wind down.

He came out to join me and asked me to pass the blunt to him. Surprising me again that night. Justin didn't usually smoke. I wasn't sure what had gotten into him, but I hoped it stayed. He stood behind me kissing on my neck in between puffs of the blunt. My phone started vibrating in my jeans pocket.

"Hold on bae. This might be important." Cassie said, as she stepped away from him. "HELLO HAVE YOU SEEN MY DAUGHTER!" A lady shouted on the other end. Cassie quickly hung up. She didn't know what the fuck to say.

"Baby who the fuck was that?" Justin worriedly asked.

She squinted at him eyes low and red from the weed. Then nervously replied, "Its Iesha's mom. How the fuck she get my number? Wat are we going to do Justin?"

"You are going to call the bitch back and act normal. Nobody knows anything. Just calm down, call her back, and see what she has to say."

"Alright I'm bout to hit her back now." Cassie shakingly returned the call, "Hello did someone just call from this number?"

"Yes I'm trying to reach my daughter Tabitha. She was supposed to come over today and take me to the doctor. She still hasn't gotten here. I'm gonna be late." The elderly lady responded.

"I'm sorry ma'am. You have the wrong number. I don't know anybody by the name." Cassie responded, with relief.

"Its ok sweetie have a nice day sorry to bother you." The lady nicely replied and hung up.

"Bitch you bout gave us both a heart attack for nothing." Justin jeered. They burst out laughing.

"It was that damn weed. Shit is some fire." Cassie acknowledged.

"Well good thing we smoked it all. Your ass don't need no more." Justin jokingly chastised.

"Well I do know what I do need." Cassie seductively whispered.

He looked at her and smiled "Oh is that right Mrs. Milton." "Excuse you. It is still Ms. Jones to you. We ain't married yet."

"Hush that fuss up and come here woman." She ran and jumped on him. They both fell backward crashing through the ajar bedroom door and onto the floor.

"This is what u want huh." Cassie flirtatiously murmured straddling Justin grinding slowly.

"You know I love the way you move those hips." He responded, overcome by lust. Someone began to bang on the bedroom door loudly.

"Go away!" Justin yelled.

"Sir its important. Somewhere is here to see you." One of the servants reported from the other side of the door.

"Tell them to go away too." He said as he was massaging Cassie's ample breasts.

"They said to tell you it's about business Sir." The help responded.

"Ughhhh I'll be down in a minute! Justin growled. "Can't ever get pussy in peace in this house I swear."

Cassie smirked and got up. "I'm getting ready for bed I'm exhausted."

"I bet you are tired, because you been drinking with the queen of the ghetto today. You think I didn't smell that Henny and loud on you when you pulled up. You can't hide shit from me. But today was a great day at the office. I didn't feel like arguing with your hard headed ass.

At least, you came back at a decent time for once. I'm going to handle this shit downstairs and handle that ass when I get back." Justin said as he grabbed her ass on his way out the door. Can't hide shit from this nigga. I might as well be in prison just without the bars. Cassie thought as she drifted off to sleep.

CHAPTER VI: SECRETS

Justin walked downstairs into the foyer. Tyrie was there waiting. "Fool what are you doing here? What if she sees you? Then she will know I'm spying on her." Justin angrily whispered.

"Look I don't care about none of that shit you talking right now. Nigga you owe me some bread. I want it right now." Tyrie demanded.

Justin motioned for Tyrie to follow him into his office. He went into his safe, handed Tyrie a couple of stacks, and then started lecturing him.

"First of you are lucky you're lucky you're my blood. I have smoked niggas for less. I don't deal with anyone just showing up at my house."

Tyrie snidely retorted, "Look I have bills to pay. I don't have time for you to pay me whenever you fucking feel like it. We have a deal. I watch your bitch and you wire money into my account every few days. It's been two weeks with nothing. I don't know what you thought this was cuz, but this ain't that."

Justin took a deep breath and exhaled slowly. "Look I don't want no beef with you. What's been going on at Tangy's? Has Tangy told her anything about the business? Is she fucking wit other niggas over there? Give me something. I'm not paying you for no reason."

Tyrie knew he had his cousin exactly where he wanted him now.

He played that tough guy shit with everybody else, but he knew better than to fuck with Tyrie. He took his time before answering Justin's line of questions.

"Cassie only goes over to Tangy's to smoke, drink, and chill. Today the first day she actually been around a whole bunch of niggas. But we just played some cards. That was it. She was so busy trying to get home to your ass that she only played one round.

You got a good girl cuz. Ain't really no need for all this."

Justin trying to keep the peace inhaled and exhaled again before responding,"I got this. Just do like I ask you to do aight. "Keep an eye on my bitch. Make sure Tangy keeps her mouth closed about what she really does for my father. I don't want Cassie to know anything, just in case anything ever goes down. Can you do that without bringing your ass back over here?"

" Yeah cuz we straight. I got you." Tyrie replied.

Justin checked the hallway to make sure nobody was in sight and slipped him out the front door.

Justin was trying to make sure that Cassie didn't discover Tyrie in the house. It would raise questions that he didn't want to answer. Because, he didn't want to lie to her anymore. Justin really loved Cassie in his own way.

He had taken more time with Tyrie than he anticipated. Cassie was probably asleep since it was well after 11 p.m. He crept up the stairs and peeped into their bedroom door. Sure, enough she had wrapped herself up under the covers. Snoring like hell. Liquor always made her snore heavily. Justin wanted nothing but to get in bed and pick up where they had left off before they got interrupted. But ravishing his beautiful fiancé would have to wait. He had business to handle.

He quickly got dressed, made a call to assemble everyone, and headed out west to The Spot. Eddie, his childhood friend, greeted him when he arrived. "Everybody is already here." Then Eddie pushed a button underneath the register. The hidden door next to the counter creaked as it slid open. Inside the door was a huge room that kind of resembled a living room. There was a huge oval table in the middle. All Justin's men were seated around the table.

"Why has my money been short the last two weeks! Don't think I haven't noticed!" Justin bellowed.

"Boss we been having problems with the Arabs. Last week they were short. This week they didn't pay at all. We roughed them up, but it still didn't help. There was hardly anything in the register. We don't know where they stashing the rest of it." One of the men answered.

"Those bastards are getting bold. I know just what to do. We will handle them tomorrow. They don't want to pay me. Then they won't open." Justin adjourned the meeting. He was satisfied that he now had an answer to his money issue. Hurriedly, he headed back out into the night to get home before his absence was detected.

Cassie rolled over. It was damn near four in the morning. Where the hell was Justin? He was always coming and going all hours of the night, when he thought she was asleep. She had become very suspicious. Cheating didn't cross her mind. He was too obsessed with her for that. It was something bigger.

First of all, no lawyer she knew walked around strapped. The other thing that made her feel uneasy was all of his family with the exception of Tangy seemed fake. His mom and dad were too seddity. Cassie had been around enough fake motherfuckers to know when they were putting on an act. She may have been young but she wasn't stupid. She decided to get out of bed instead of lying there overthinking.

Cassie got up to have a glass of wine and roll up. She had been drinking and smoking a lot more since the deaths of Iesha and Donte. Losing them really made her feel all alone. She wondered why her mother hadn't reached out all. She had expected her to at least want money or something. But she hadn't asked her for anything or acted like she cared that she was even alive.

Carrying around all this pain was eating away at Cassie slowly. So much had happened in the last year. Hell, most of her life had been a nightmare. If she was really being honest with herself. The only bright spot she ever had was her father. But, if her own Daddy would just leave why should she expect any other nigga to treat her better.

She definitely didn't want a bitch. Being with a female never appealed to her in the least. She wanted somebody big and strong to make her feel protected. Not somebody with the same anatomy as her that she would probably feel obligated to protect. She couldn't even wrap her mind around the idea of bumping coochies or getting fucked with a strap.

Hell, she had toys. She could get her own self off before it came down to that.

She finished rolling her blunt and stepped on the balcony to clear her head and smoke. The cool night breeze was refreshing. She watched the smoke as it floated up into the air. Justin zoomed into the driveway taking her attention from her latest smoke cloud. He most likely didn't notice her because she was standing in the shadows. The light from the motion detectors couldn't reach her silhouette.

Another vaguely familiar car pulled in behind him a few seconds later. A tall light skin figure stepped out. It was Tyrie. What the hell was he doing there? Cassie wondered. She decided to put the blunt out so that the smoke didn't alert anyone to her presence outside. She didn't want Justin to know that she was onto the funny shit that he had going on.

Tomorrow she decided she would go see Tangy to get some answers. Something told her that she could trust Tangy more than anyone. She went inside and got back into bed just in case Justin decided to come into the house. Thinking about her mission the following day, Cassie dozed off. The blunt and drink had hit her a lot quicker than she anticipated.

Donte's phone rang instantly waking him up out of his sleep. He rolled over with his eyes still closed and felt for it on the night stand. Groggily answering, "Nigga do u know what time it is? What the fuck do you want? I thought our business was done.

Coming down to ATL, confessing, and you supposedly killing me was supposed to be it. I held up to my end I haven't contacted Cassie. She's all alone and all yours what more do you want?" He questioned Justin.

"Look lil nigga don't forget I own you. Do you want all your baby cousin's family wiped out in their sleep? I will make good on my promise." Justin ranted.

"Get to the damn point. I do have other shit to do besides sit on the phone with you in the middle of the night." Donte said, trying to speed Justin along to the point of the call.

"Did you take care of Iesha's mom. Some woman called Cassie today. I think it was her."

Donte responded to Justin in disbelief. "Nigga you woke me up for this. That bitch been on fucking Pluto since she got out. Zooted like a motherfucker. Guess some addicts just can't re-form."

Justin released a sigh of relief. "What about Cassie's mom? What's her deal? Is she still looking for her?"

Donte was exasperated by this point by Justin's seemingly endless questions. "It seems like you don't know shit for a nigga that's supposed to have a lot of connections."

"There was a memorial service for Cassie. The police just gave up on her case saying they presumed she was dead. I'm sure that had something to do with you. But anyway, her moms capped herself and the nigga she was fucking a few days later. People say she did it because of guilt. They say she let all those men fuck on Cassie to keep her bills paid. You know how folks in the hood talk.

"This convo never happened. I just needed to make sure everything was good." Justin hung up as quickly as he called.

"Who was that Donte?" Iesha sat up in bed and asked.

"The psycho that has your best friend." He responded.

"I hate that bastard. We were doing just fine. Why he felt like he had to do all this bullshit? I just don't get it.

"Oh, you know why." Donte smugly responded. "Anybody related to Joe's ass has to be a little crazy. He is his nephew after all. It's got to run in the bloodline. Those niggas don't think like the rest of us. I did meet him back in the day when we were younger. He was small and nerdy. Never thought he grow up to be a drug kingpin. I wish like hell we never got Cassie tangled in all this mess Iesha."

"I wish we weren't in this mess either. Now we over here playing dead and shit" Iesha snapped. But she had just gotten the life she always wanted to have to leave it behind. It was hard having to start completely over again. She missed her kids and her siblings with every fiber of her being. Being away from them was the only way to keep them safe. Luckily, she had enough money to pay someone to take care of them until this fiasco was over. She would play the lunatic's game for now. It couldn't last forever.

Justin had abruptly ended his call with Donte when he saw Tyrie pull up behind him.

He jumped out angrily to see what he wanted, "Nigga didn't I tell you not to come over here again!" Justin yelled.

"Well somebody stole the stash from Tangy's. They went in with pistols and shit. I didn't want to call because I don't know what's what right now. Tangy is shook up like a motherfucker. We need to get on this shit asap. What u want me to do!" Tyrie exclaimed.

"Calm your ass down. We have to be smart about this. Call everybody now. Tell them to meet us at The Spot again. These assholes know better than to steal from me. We have to handle this shit immediately.

"Alright bet" Tyrie said. Then he got on his phone, a jumped into his car, and screeched down the street. Justin leaped back in his SUV and followed behind him. They reached the spot in record time. Tyrie and Justin walked in to see everyone sitting at tables out front. It was early morning. Nobody would see them so they thought.

"Boss how u want to handle this? Thugga, Justin right hand man next to Tyrie, spoke up immediately.

"Damn let me get in the door good first. I need a drink. Eddie do ya'll have any liquor in this motherfucker?"

His best friend brought him a bottle of Henny and a shot glass. Justin poured it, chugged it, and exhaled slowly. "Alright we gotta get these motherfuckers. Y'all said you were having problems with the Arabs. No doubt it was them. I was going to handle this shit later today. But fuck that let's do it right now. We are about to burn all their shit to the ground. I am the king of Georgia. Ain't nobody bout to fuck with me like this."

"Are you going to call your father first. Because this shit bout to start a war?" Tyrie asked concerned.

"No fuck him. I got this. I ain't asking for approval for a mother fucking thing. These motherfuckers tried to send a message by stealing my shit. We about to return it. Just go do what I said." Everyone hustled out the door after Justin's last words.

Even in the midst of all this chaos Justin was still thinking about Cassie. He stayed behind to briefly talk to Eddie. "Close this place early tonight. I'm bringing Cassie in for a private dinner. She has been acting kind of funky lately. I want to smooth everything over. You know I love that bitch.

"Yeah, you shooting that gun off in here was pretty crazy. Then having me take them straight to the airport. I'm used to your antics but this one takes the cake. Jay all this shit is new to her. Maybe being able to talk to her friends would help her nerves calm down some." Eddie suggested.

"Nah man, I want her to cut all ties from the past. I don't want her getting nostalgic and want to take a trip back home. This is the best way to keep her in Georgia with me. I'm all she has now." Justin explained.

"Are you sure you can trust Tyrie watching her?" Eddie asked.

"Yeah man. You know that's the only blood I do trust. Him and Tangy are like my brother and sister instead of cousins. They were at our house more than their own until Dad started beefing with Uncle Joe.

"But nigga how you gon kill your own uncle over a bitch?" Eddie asked while shaking his head.

"Joe had gone too far. It was time to put his ass down. Dad was mad about it. But he got over it. True love only strikes once. The first time I saw her I knew she had to be mine by any means necessary. Enough about this shit. It's already over and done. I need to get my ass home before Cassie wakes up.

I have been gone half the night and still look like yesterday. Last thing I want is for her to think I'm stepping out. You know she has trust issues because of everything that she been through." Justin said standing up.

"Alright man. We gon catch up later. Be careful. You got a lot of shit going on and its just getting worse. You my homie for life. I'm just tryna look out for you." Eddie said.

Justin turned and looked over his shoulder as he was heading to the door, "I will hit you up later with the rest of the details for tonight. I have so much other shit to deal with that I can't focus on dinner right now."

"Peace God" Eddie said to his friend as he departed.

"Oh, you Muslim nigga." Justin replied.

Eddie just laughed. Justin headed back home for the second time. Unknowingly taking a whole heap of trouble with him.

Justin was cuddled up to Cassie when she awakened. Her stomach turned when she looked at him lying next to her. He woke up and caught her staring at him. He missed the look of disgust on her face. "Good morning beautiful" he said before he kissed her forehead. She kissed him back. The wave a nausea hit her again.

After what she had seen last night, being intimate with him just felt weird as fuck and made her sick to her stomach. She thought she had some idea of who she was dealing with, but now she knew that she was totally in the dark about everything.

If her mind was ever going to be at ease, she had to get to Tangy's to get some answers. Luckily, Justin seemed to be in a rush that morning. He got up and got dressed and headed straight out the door. Cassie rushed to Tangy's as soon as she thought the coast was clear. It was early as fuck but she couldn't wait another minute. Tangy would probably still be asleep.

Cassie banged on the door like the police when she arrived at her friend's home. Tangy opened the door wide eyed with sleep still in the corners of her eyes.

"Girl what the hell are you doing here? It's eight in the morning. Is something wrong?"

Cassie quickly began speaking of her concerns. "I saw Tyrie at my house last night. I had no idea he knew Justin. It's really got me shook. He's usually here when I visit. I figured you would know the scoop. Just tell me whatever it is Tangy. I feel like you're the only one I can trust right now."

Tangy looked conflicted for a moment before she responded. "Well, get your ass off my porch. Come in and have breakfast. I'll tell you everything. You're a good girl Cassie. Different than the others that my cousin has dealt with before. I don't want to see your life ruined. I'm in too deep. But, there's still a chance for you." The phone rang cutting Tangy off.

Cassie watched the look of shock on her friend's face. The phone conversation ended quickly.

Immediately Tangy warned Cassie. "Tyrie is dead! Go home and get your shit now! Leave and never look back! You have to get out of my house now!"

Cassie begged, "Please, finish telling me what you were going to say before the phone rang." "Nah I love, I can't get in this shit. I'm not trying to end up dead too." She grabbed Cassie by the arm and gently pushed her out the house. Then slammed and locked the door.

Cassie walked slowly to her car. Disappointed that she didn't get any answers. She knew Tangy was right. That she should just go. But she was tired of running. Hell, running is how she ended up with Justin in the first place. If Tangy wouldn't give her the answers, she would find them another way. She decided that she needed protection so she began to google local pawn shops. Once she found one nearby, she pulled out of Tangy's driveway and headed in that direction.

After Tangy kicked Cassie out, she called her uncle back. "Cassie doesn't know anything. Justin just got really sloppy and made her suspicious. I didn't tell her anything and followed your instructions. She should be on her way home to pack and leave now. Justin should have known better than to bring her here in the first place. Do you think it's because she looks like Mara? I think that's why he has done all this."

I think he still blames himself for Mara's death." Richard sighed, "This is partly my fault. I shouldn't have let Joe use him in the first place. He was soft to deal with the girls. I have pressing business to attend. I'll call you later with more instructions. You know we have this Arab situation to straighten out. Baby girl you know you're my favorite niece. I count on you."

She teasingly replied, "That's because I'm your only niece." Richard laughed heartily. "I love you Tangy."

"Love you too Unc." Tangy hung up and decided to go back to bed. She figured her day was bound to get better the second time around.

Richard hung up the phone satisfied that everything was going according to plan. Justin could get back on track without Cassie in the way. She had been making him lose focus. The elder Mr. Milton was tired of cleaning up his son's messes. This war with the Arabs was the last straw. He was willing use Joe's murder as leverage with his son to get him to fall in line if he resisted. Richard had full confidence that he had his son exactly where he wanted him now.

Justine walked into his office interrupting his thoughts. "Richard what are you doing up so early? I thought u were taking today off."

"Woman you know there are no days off for somebody in my line of work" Richard haughtily answered.

"You are the hardest working lawyer. I've ever seen honey." Justine sweetly responded.

Richard gave his wife a warm smile. He took pride in the fact that he kept the true nature of the business away from Justine all these years. He thought she was very naïve. Perhaps he shouldn't have underestimated his wife. It's always the ones closest to you that end up causing the most damage.

Justine walked out of her husband's office and back upstairs.

Thinking about the entire conversation, she had just overheard. It wasn't the first. She had heard several throughout the years. Since, her husband could never really hear her light footsteps approaching his office door. She decided this time she wouldn't stand idly by. It was Cassie's resemblance to Mara that sprung her into action. She couldn't save her daughter in time. But she was determined to rescue Cassie.

Before Justine left to pay Cassie an impromptu visit, she rummaged around in her underwear drawer until she found the manilla folder hidden underneath her panties. She had been gathering evidence for years against her husband. The folder contained enough evidence to put Richard away for two lifetimes. Justine hadn't found the right time to use it until now.

She had wanted to take it and leave after Mara died. She had discovered it was her deceitful husband and his trifling brother's fault that her sweet girl was dead. She only stayed out of fear for the rest of her family. She had overheard Richard tell Joe that he would go after them all if she ever left him. Justine knew he was a very powerful man. She didn't want to put her family through that type of anguish.

There was nothing for her to be scared of any longer. She was determined to save herself and Cassie from the Milton men. Justine strolled out to her Mercedes and started the long drive to her son's estate.

The drive to Justin's place didn't seem to take as long as usual. Justine was pleased to spot Cassie sitting on the steps in front of the house. She had been afraid she may have still been out. The girl appeared disheveled. Justine could smell the blunt Cassie was attempting to put out behind her back. Surprisingly Justine told her to pass.

"No need to put it out. After everything you have been through, I would be smoking too. Pass it here. I think I need some too. Come walk with me. We have a lot to discuss." Cassie hit the blunt again and passed it. She followed Justine in the direction of the flower garden and gazebo. They walked in silence for a while just passing the blunt back and forth. Justine was gathering her thoughts and Cassie was freaking the fuck out. What could Justin's mom possibly have to say to her she wondered.

They finally got to the gazebo and sat down. Cassie was a little out of breath. She stared at Justine catching her breath. She didn't know if she was high or what but she thought Justin's mom kinda resembled Claire Huxtable.

Justine stared back intently at Cassie for a moment. "You are such a really beautiful girl come sit by me. You don't have to sit all the way over there. I don't bite I promise." Cassie laughed and obliged. They smoked the rest of the blunt side by side. Justine suddenly grabbed Cassie's hand. Cassie jumped startled.

"Don't be afraid. Here I have something to show you. Justine pulled the manilla folder out of her Berkin bag. "What's all this? Cassie questioned.

"I'll get to that in a moment. I want to tell u a story. I guess we can start with this flower garden and gazebo. This garden was not just planted here to look nice. It was planted as a memorial for a very sweet girl that looked exactly like you. She loved sunflowers. So, it was only right that we planted them in her honor.

I'm sure you're wondering what happened to the girl. Well, she's right here with us. This is why neither Richard or I ever come out here. The guilt is just too much. I've been hiding this secret for years. But seeing your face has made me finally want to break my silence."

Cassie stared at Justine in a daze. She heard what she was saying but she felt she must be tripping. There is no way this lady just told her that they were sitting on top of a dead body.

Justine continued. "Many years ago, I went into this bar with my friends. There was this blues band playing. I saw the finest chocolate man I've ever seen in my life on the stage playing the saxophone. Well, I made it my business to get his number. I was determined not to leave that bar without it.

If I knew then what I know now I would have just taken my fast ass home." Cassie chuckled.

"As you surely have guessed by now that man was Richard.

Richard and I had a world wind romance. We were married within four months. I had Justin first. Then a year later, Mara. Justin was named after me of course. Richard argued about the name at first, but eventually gave in. Mara, we named after my mother. Y'all could be twins. You look so much alike." Cassie gasped in surprise as the dots began to connect in her mind. Justine continued her story gazing off into the flowerbeds.

"We struggled from time to time, but we were happy. I had my intelligent boy, beautiful girl, and handsome husband. Richard and I both had jobs. I was a sales clerk at a local department store. Richard was a musician.

He got paid to play that horn every night in a local club. We even owned our own home. I felt I had everything I ever wanted. Everything was perfect until Richard's brother Joe came to town." Cassie's eyes got wide as she continued to listen.

"Joe was one smooth talking fancy dressing nigga. Much different than my Richard. Joe talked Richard into quitting music and joining his organization. The Firm is what he called it. They wore tailored suits everywhere they went and had some prominent friends. People just assumed since they called themselves The Firm that they were actual lawyers.

So, the firm became Milton and Associates. They even went as far as to hire real lawyers to take cases. Richard and Joe didn't have a degree the first second or third but when we moved here nobody knew that. The business was already established and the lie kept going.

Richard doesn't think I know til this day. I went rummaging in his office one day. I get these feelings sometimes. Something just told me to do it. I found most of that stuff that's in that envelope I just gave you. That's how I know all this. I don't know all the particulars of how their influential friends helped them turn a drug organization into a law firm. But they did it. These niggas are slicker than oil." Cassie laughed.

"Where was I. So, besides The Firm Joe owned The Lion's Den Gentleman's Club. Which of course you're aware. I do believe that's where my son found you. I gathered that eavesdropping on a conversation between my husband and son the night you turned up with him at our house. Cassie looked down. "Don't be ashamed chile. I've done some stuff in my day too. But that's another story for another day. Back to the story at hand.

The club is how Joe trafficked, drugs, guns, and girls overseas. It was also a brothel. Athletes from far n wide liked to go and sample the finest girls that Joe had to offer. He had some kind of deal with a lot of the team owners. They used The Den to keep their players happy and out of the tabloids. As you can see, Richard and Joe had a lucrative business empire going.

A few years ago, they got too greedy. They made made a two-million-dollar deal with some men in China to deliver girls and drugs. It was too much for them to deliver, and they did the unthinkable to get out of trouble with the men. The men gave Richard and Joe a choice of returning the money and never working with them again or sacrificing something they loved a great deal. Those two selfish greedy bastards didn't want to go back to being poor, so they sacrificed my babies."

"What! Cassie exclaimed. Justine reluctantly resumed her tale. It was hard for her to actually put into words how malicious the two men had been.

"I had misplaced my keys and was going to Richard's office to ask him if he had seen them. He had the phone on speakerphone. I stood in the hallway to listen as I usually did. That's the only way I could get the truth in that house. I heard a Chinese man's voice ask him if the kids were in place and he responded yes. Then the line went dead. A few hours later my Mara was murdered and Justin was in the hospital fighting for his life.

When Justin got out the hospital, he decided to join his dad's organization. He felt like is he was man enough to take a bullet then he could deal with working for his Dad. Richard didn't want him to do it. But Joe talked Richard into bringing Justin in. He wanted use my son to attract girls to bring to The Den to work and sell. When Justin found out girls were being sold, he wanted out. His father paid for him to get on the team. That's how he became the baller you met."

Cassie reflected back to the story Donte had told her about how Joe planned for months to get her to The Den. It all made sense now. Justine was filling in the blanks for her. She broke away from her thoughts and kept listening.

"I love my son. But he's very sick. He hasn't been right since Mara's death. I believe that's what lead him to kill his own uncle to save you. He wanted to protect you. The way he couldn't protect my sweet Mara. I think he still feels guilty that he survived and she didn't. I guess knowing all this you're wondering why I'm still with Richard. I overheard him tell Joe he would kill me dead and everything I hold dear if I ever left. Now that my family is safely away or died of old age, it's my chance to be free of this mess. I want you to break free too.

I'm about to get as far away from here as possible. That's why I'm telling you all this. The folder you have isn't the only copy. The FBI and local police have the other copies. My son and his father are going down. Joe would be going down too, if Justin hadn't killed him. I rather see them both behind bars than for them to destroy anyone else's life.

I told you the story and gave you the folder as proof I wasn't lying. I want you to understand how much danger you're truly in. Get as far away from this place as you can Cassie and never look back."

The women embraced. Justine walked back to her car, waved good bye, and drove off. Cassie sat at the gazebo and mulled over the contents of the folder. All the pictures, bank statements, deeds, etc backed up everything Justine had just said. She pulled her sack out her pocket and rolled up again. This was a lot of shit to digest at once.

She was glad she had purchased the gun. It made her feel safer knowing what she did now. The only real question was where the fuck was she going to go. Just then her phone rang. She dropped it in shock. It was definitely a surprise who was on the other end.

"Girl I thought you were dead. Cassie sobbed."

Iesha responded, There's so much I have to tell you. I hope that you're sitting down." Cassie wasn't sure was ready for more news after the conversation she just had with Justine. But, here was her best friend alive and well. She decided to hear her out.

"I know you're shocked. But I had to make sure you were alright. I couldn't take not knowing anymore. I feel so much better now that I've heard your voice. Obviously, I'm not dead like you thought. Donte isn't either. That crazy motherfucker Justin threatened us into to pretending to be dead. He said that it was the only way to get you to forget the past and move on with him.

He threatened to kill my whole fam if me and Donte didn't come down there to the restaurant. We didn't found out that he planned to make us disappear until after we got down there. I really didn't want to do this but what choice did I have. Donte agreed because I'm all he has left. Justin just shot two rounds in the air after you walked out. Then he went running out to scare you like something had happened. His homeboy Eddie drove us to the airport and handed us tickets to fucking Africa. Bitch I'm on some Island near there."

Cassie interrupted,"What do we do now. I've got to get away from his crazy ass."

Iesha instructed, "Get you a passport, get your ass down here, and we will figure it all out. Just call me before you leave and I'll make arrangements on this end. I told Donte I was just coming to the mainland to pick up a few things. I've got to go or he will get suspicious. He will kill me if he knew I made contact."

Cassie had one question for her friend before she hung up. "Iesha how did you get my number?"

She hurriedly responded "My mother." Then hung up.

Cassie finished smoking, left the gazebo, and started walking towards the house. Justin was pulling up just has she approached the front steps. She quickly took the folder that was in her hands and tucked it underneath her shirt. She knew Justin would go berserk if he saw that shit.

She gave him a small wave. Then she went inside, heading straight for the bathroom. She found herself puking again. It was crazy how just the sight of him was making her so damn nauseous all of a sudden.She hid the envelope in her vanity under her makeup. Justin would never find it in there. She washed her face in cold water. Then came out prepared to face Justin but he wasn't inside.

She went outside and peered over the balcony. His truck was gone again. That was weird. But this is Justin we're talking about. She was relieved he left. It gave her more time to plan her next move. Her phone vibrated. It was a text from Justin that told her something to put something sexy on and meet him at The Spot. He said he had a surprise waiting for her. The last thing she wanted to do was visit that restaurant again. But she didn't want him to get suspicious. She showered, changed, and headed to the restaurant where a bigger surprise was waiting than she anticipated.

CHAPTER VII : THE END OF THE ROAD

The task force leader stood in front of the bulletin board looking at the pictures of Richard, Justin, and all their known associates. The manilla folder still was laying on his desk. Tonight, was the night he had been anticipating for over five years. Thanks to the mysterious envelope that had arrived by messenger with no return address earlier that day.

He still couldn't believe it contained all the information to put The Firm out of business for good. The FBI had tried many times before to shut down the organization, but Richard was like Mr. Untouchable. His pockets ran deep and he was able to slip through their fingers every time. But not this time. Their case would be solid.

The other task force members slowly began to stroll in.

Mullins began to brief them while they put on their gear. "We got intel that Richard will be home tonight. His son will be at that shady restaurant with his fiancé. We're going to hit them both at the same time. They will never see it coming. Jasper how did your surveillance go?"

" As y'all know we have been tailing Justin for weeks. Last night after our boys rattled his cousin Tangy, he went straight to The Spot with our informant Tyrie. We were able to hear from the wire that Tyrie was wearing that The Firm thought the Arabs were responsible for what happened at Tangy's place.

We were also clearly able to hear Justin give the order for the arson. Here is the recording from that wire and the photos from the restaurant. Justin is clearly seen entering and existing in the early morning hours. We then followed the suspects and watched as some of the crew burned one of the Arab stores to the ground in retaliation.

Since we were ordered not to engage only collect evidence, here are all the photos from the store incident. You can clearly see the plates on all the vehicles involved. We ran the plates through our system. All off them belong to Richard. Why he purchased cars for his gang members, I will never understand but it makes our job easier. These other pictures show the faces of all the crew members that took part in the arson."

Mullins interrupted, "Thank you Jasper. We had enough thanks to Jasper's team and that envelope on my desk to get search warrants for the restaurant and the homes of Justin and Richard. We're moving now before anyone has a chance to give them a heads up. Somebody in this bureau has been feeding them information. That's why I called you all tonight personally. I knew nobody could leak the information to them that way. It has to be one of the higher ups. But we will worry about that problem later. Everyone ready?" The team all nodded their heads yes.

"Lets move!" Mullins ordered. The agents hurried to their respective vehicles. They cars split up after leaving headquarters to arrest all the suspects at once. The Miltons were not going to recover from this

Justine took one last look around her home in which she had spent most of her youth and most of her formidable years. She grabbed her few bags that she had packed with her favorite outfits and the majority of the money from the safe. She glanced at all the pictures of her family along the walls as she made her way down the staircase one last time. Richard was locked in the office. He wasn't aware of her impeding departure. She had paid all the staff earlier and told them to take the evening off. Despite everything she Richard in her own way. Maybe it was Stockholm syndrome but she wanted him to go out with some type of dignity. His terrible deeds would be made public soon enough.

She had thought long and hard before she sent Agent Mullins that envelope with everything the police needed to put her husband and son away. But it was past time for all this business to be over. Too many had gotten hurt and her precious daughter deserved justice.

Justine didn't regret her decision as she placed her things into her trunk, got into her Mercedes, and headed off to the airport for parts unknown. She had boarded her plane and was in the air well before the police arrived at her house.

Cassie was nervous. She had only handled a gun once before. But she was ready for anything, Justin pulled that evening. Her gun was in a holster on her side under her jacket. She had decided on wearing fitted jeans and thigh high Timbs that had been custom made. Her outfit had been planned out carefully.

Cassie wanted to not be restricted in case she needed to fight or protect herself at the restaurant. When she arrived, she saw cop cars out front. Justin was being put in the back of one of the cars in handcuffs. She decided to play her role just in case Justin managed to walk that night. Cassie hopped out her car screaming, What's going on! What are you doing with my fiancé?"

Justin assured her that he would be out by morning. He told her to go home look in his rolodex on his office table and call his lawyer.

Cassie ran back to her car and sped towards the house. Not to call the lawyer but to get her shit. This was her chance to escape. She had no idea where the hell she was going or who to call. Tangy's name popped in her head for some reason. Cassie called her as she was racing back home to get her things.

Tangy answered on the second ring. "Girl they got Justin. Now's my chance. I'm grabbing some clothes, but I have no idea where the hell to go."

Tangy responded, "Forget them damn clothes. Come over here right now. I got you. I knew this was going to happen." Cassie made a u- turn and sped to Tangy's place.

Justin and Richard arrived at the police station simultaneously. Their lawyer was already there ready to fight for the men's release.

Richard had the foresight to call him when he heard the FBI banging on his front door.

Justin was handcuffed to a chair outside the interview room. While Richard was lead inside first by Mullins. Their lawyer quickly followed behind. The door closed and the interrogation began. Mullins was leading it with Lopez as his backup. The other members of the task force watched the interrogation from the other side of the glass. They were giddy with excitement that they had finally landed their big fish.

Mullins took out the manilla folder and spread all the evidence on the desk. Richards looked like he was about to shit on himself. He had a look of absolute disgust across his face. Whoever the hell had betrayed him like this would pay. Mullins smirked at Richard's look of outrage.

"Your name is everywhere. However, your son's is barely mentioned. Besides the pictures from the fire last night. We have nothing on him. He will go away on arson and that's it. When we bring him in this room, I'm sure he will sing like a canary."

Lopez whispered in Mullins ear. Then Mullins continued his interrogation. "Scratch that we found remains on your son's property. Also, several suspicious payments to the Canary Islands. It's only a matter of time before we find out who those payments went to. How about you save yourself from life with no possibility of parole and fill in the blanks Richard."

His lawyer spoke up, "Don't say anything. We don't know the source of this evidence. This could all be fake." Richard looked down and just held his head. He wasn't built for jail and his son wasn't either. There had to be a way out this mess but what. Richard refused to say anything. Mullins got annoyed and sent him to holding to await his bond hearing.

Justin was ushered in after Richard was out of sight. "Have a seat Mr. Milton. As you can see, you're in some pretty big trouble." Mullins motioned to the pictures of him at the restaurant. Then he played the recording of him directing the crew. Then to add insult to injury Mullins tossed the pictures of his sister's remains, that they had unearthed from under the gazebo onto the table.

Justin lost it when he saw the photos of his sister and started crying. Mullins wasn't expecting that. Most guys in the game he brought in were tough. But Justin was different. He definitely wasn't built for this gangster lifestyle. Justin wiped his eyes on his sleeve.

"You're fired." Justin said to his lawyer after he was done crying.

The lawyer asked, "Are you sure?"

Justin hollered, "Yes! Get Out!" Justin agreed to tell Mullins everything after the lawyer left. But, only under the condition that Mullins put in writing that Justin had complete immunity. Mullins thought about it for a minute then reluctantly agreed. He left Justin in the interrogation room to start the paperwork.

Justin just sat their teary eyed and scared. He knew if his father managed to get out that he would kill him son or no son. Justin thought maybe that wouldn't be such a bad thing and relaxed a little bit. At least then he would be with his beloved sister Mara again. She always took such good care of her big brother. She helped him on his darkest days. A shrink that he had seen once, told him that his attachment to Mara was unhealthy and borderline obsessive. But Justin felt it was just a close bond that he shared with his sister that most people didn't understand.

Cassie was the only person that had made him happy since Mara was murdered. She got him and he loved that about her. Justin figured she was long gone by now. He couldn't blame her after the way he had acted. But if he did manage to skate on this mess, he vowed to get her back.

Tangy ran up to Cassie's car and jumped into the passenger seat as soon as as she drove up. "Where are we going?" Cassie nervously questioned.

Tangy quickly responded, "We're going to see a friend that's going to give us everything we need to get far away from here. Stop asking questions and just drive." Tangy directed Cassie to one of the suburbs near her home. She stopped her when they reached a medium size brick house. One of the finest men Cassie had ever seen immediately opened the door and invited them into the home.

"Come in. I've been expecting you two." He warmly said. The women hurriedly entered and Tangy made introductions.

"Cassie this is my best friend Shawn. He is the best forger that I know." Shawn handed them each a passport. "Pay the man so we can get going." Tangy instructed. Cassie paid Shawn and the pair headed back to the car.

Cassie had more questions. "Where are we going now?"

Tangy replied, "We are going to the airport. The Canary Islands to be exact. I found out exactly where your friends are located. We are going to join them. The next flight to Morocco is in two hours. Once we land there will be a speed boat waiting. The boat will take us to the island where Iesha and Donte will be waiting."

Cassie drove quietly for a moment then asked, "Tangy, why are you doing all this? How did you get it all set up so fast?"

Tangy got this melancholy look on her face before she replied, "This is my penance. I didn't help Mara when she came to me for answers. I was too scared of Uncle Richard to help. Then she went to Justin's and got murdered. We had a small burial for her after it happened. Aunt Justine, Uncle Richard, Tyrie, Justin, and I were the only ones there. It's haunted me ever since.

You rushing into my house today gave me the feeling of deja vu. Mara had the same expression on her face the day she came over. Part of the reason I befriended you was because you look just like her. It was like having a piece of her back again.

After you left, I soul searched for a while. I decided that I wasn't going to let my Uncle take you away like he did Mara. I called the police and left an anonomous tip where Mara was buried. Then I called Shawn to get everything ready. I knew you would be calling. Justin had you so isolated where else would you turn. I'm going to make sure you get to your friends safely. Then I'm parting ways. If anyone is looking for me, I don't want them to find you too."

Cassie and Tangy arrived at the airport in record time. They had no bags so it was a breeze to purchase their tickets, get through security, and find their gate. The women sat anxiously waiting for their boarding call. Cassie glanced around nervously. She spotted Iesha walking towards her through the crowd. Cassie ran over to immediately to find out what the hell she was doing there.

She slowed her pace and started backing away slowly when saw Tyrie behind her. What in the entire hell was going on. Cassie thought to herself. It was funny how people had a way of coming back from the dead dealing with this family.

Tyrie spoke first. "Tangy you need to get as far away as possible."

Tangy suspiciously asked, "How do you know? Uncle Richard said that you were dead." She trusted her cousin about as much as she did her uncle at this point.

"I've been helping the police to build a case against Unc and Justin. They want you to get away from here and us three to testify. That's why Iesha and I are here. They figured Cassie would trust us enough to come with us to the safe house. There's a car waiting outside."

Tangy still had more questions. "Why can't I come? Why did Unc tell me you were dead, Why the hell did you get involved with the police in the first place?"

Tyrie sighed annoyed, "Look we really don't have time for all these damn questions Tangy. The police think it's safer if you don't come with us. You're their ace in the hole if anything happens to us. Uncle Richard didn't know he was lying when he told you I was dead.

I had to fake my own death because of everything that went down last night. I've been in protective custody every since.

The reason I started helping the police was because Justin and Uncle Richard needed to be stopped. I was tired of them running our lives. Looking at Cassie's face all the time; I just couldn't sit around and do nothing anymore. Now can we get the hell out of here."

Boarding for the plane to Morocco was announced over the loud speaker. Cassie instantly hugged Tangy tightly. She had been Cassie's rock in this madness with Justin. Tangy started boarding her flight, turned and waved. Then she disappeared out of sight.

Iesha, Tyrie, and Cassie hurried outside to the awaiting town car. They headed to the place this mess all started. Cassie got alarmed when she recognized where they were going. She worriedly asked, "Why are going to Joe's country estate?"

"Donte told me about this place. I told the police this is where I wanted to come. Nobody will ever think to look for us out here" Iesha explained.

"Speaking of Donte, where is he?" Cassie asked her best friend.

"He made a deal that he would tell the Feds everything they needed to know about the Lion's Den. His stipulations were that they didn't charge him and let him stay on the island. They agreed to his terms because they needed his information to find some missing girls."

"What are you doing here?" Cassie asked Iesha puzzled.

"You're my best friend. I'm not going to let you face this shit alone. I got you. There's something else I have to tell u too. My mom somehow tracked me down after Donte got her out of jail. I'm sorry Cassie but she said your mom killed herself. I know you had your differences, but that was still your mother."

Iesha only knew parts of the abuse I endured at mom's house. I wasn't sad my Mom was dead. I know that sounds bad but I wasn't. I could finally move on with my life and bury all the pain she caused with her.

The car finally stopped. We had finally reached my old prison as I called it. Mullins stepped out of his unmarked car where he had been waiting and greeted us. "I know you all have been through a great deal. This will all be over soon. The Attorney General is expediating the trial. All this will be over in a couple of weeks just sit tight.

We have left supplies to get you through tonight. Tomorrow someone will bring everything you need for the upcoming weeks. Guards are posted at the entrance leading to this place. Y'all are safe." Mullins drove off. They went inside, chose rooms, and drifted off to restless sleep. The ordeal had been tough, but it was almost over.

Richard paced back and forth in his cell wondering what the hell was taking his son so long in the interrogation room. They had a lot to discuss before the arraignment in the morning. His lawyer approached his cell. "What happened? Where's my son!" Richard exclaimed, as soon as he caught sight of his attorney.

"He fired me. I believe he is making a deal. I don't think you will be seeing him. I'll be in touch." His lawyer turned his back and walked away. Richard punched the wall. How could his future heir do this to him. There would be hell to pay. Nobody crossed a Milton. Blood or not.

Justin was sitting in front of the station contemplating his next move. The questions Mullins had asked were tough. But he had answered every one. He didn't give the agent any more information than was asked. But it was still enough to put his father away for a long time. He needed to talk to his Mom. She always comforted him in times of crisis. Justin dialed her number and it went straight to voicemail. He sat for a moment about what to do next.

Justin's world had been turned upside down in one night. All his money was gone. The Feds seized everything that had his name on it. All his family seemed to be gone too. There was only one person that he could think of that would still help him.

He decided to call Eddie. Justin was sure that his best friend would let him crash at his place. Eddie picked up the phone on the second ring, "Hey man I was worried about you. This shit is all over the news."

Justin reassured him, "I'm cool man. I just need a place to crash until I sort this all out. Can you come pick up from the police station?"

"Yeah man I got you. I'll be there in a few minutes." Justin sat and gazed off into space until his buddy arrived.

Cassie woke up in a state of disbelief about what had transpired. She laid in bed trying to get her bearings before she got up to get dressed. Iesha knocked on her door, came in, and sat at the edge of her bed. Stroking her long ebony tresses.

"You ok bestie. You have been through hell and back. I know it has to be hitting you hard by now."

Cassie just began sobbing. Iesha just rubbed her back and let her cry it all out. She cried for her innocence that she lost at the hand of her mother's boyfriends and everything else that had lead to this moment.

Tyrie came in and broke up the sentiment. "Ya'll better suck this shit up. We not doing this today. The girls looked at him and rolled their eyes.

Cassie looked at him a longer than she should have. He caught her gaze and began grinning. Iesha sensed the vibes between them and excused herself.

Tyrie went over and sat beside Cassie. "Did I ask you to sit down nigga. Get out my room."

Tyrie coolly responded. "Girl stop your mess. You looking at me like I'm a bottle of water and you're dehydrated out in the desert."

Cassie rolled her eyes. "I don't remember you being this damn corny at Tangy's house."

"So, you were checking for a brother then. Don't even think about rolling those big brown eyes at me. You know I'm right." Tyrie smugly responded.

"You aight." Cassie said grinning.

"There it is. That big pretty smile I saw when I first met you." Tyrie flirtingly stated. They chatted some more before Cassie kicked him out so she could go get dressed.

After she was done, the three sat down to breakfast. Iesha had cooked while Justin and Cassie had been in her room flirting. "Don't think I'm bout to do this shit every day. Y'all asses gon cook too."

"Girl we hear you. When we getting out of here anyway. I been couped up in this place one time. I'm not real excited to be here again." Cassie said.

"They said in a few weeks when they dropped the supplies off earlier. They coming here the day before court to prep us for the stand." Tyrie answered.

Eddie promptly went to get his friend. Justin walked to the car before he could even pull into a parking spot. He was so ready to get away from the precinct. "Are you hungry or anything? We can make a stop before we get back to the house." Eddie asked.

"Nah I'm good. Is my stuff still in my old room from when I stayed with you, while they were finishing up my spot?" Justin inquired.

"Yeah, everything is where you left it." Eddie answered.

"Aight bet. I'm just gon shower and crash today has been hell of a day." Justin said.

"Say less bruh I got you."Eddie continued chatting. "You know they got my pops too. Mom going crazy. They talking bout putting him away for life. I know some of the shit y'all was into but I didn't know it was that deep. They didn't mess with me. You know I only ran the restaurant and that was it."

"Yo pull ova right here." Justin said cutting his friend off mid-sentence. Eddie pulled over at the appliance store.

Justin walked up to the window and continued to watch the broadcast that caught his attention. Richard, Eddie's dad, and Justin's face were on the screen. He couldn't believe how the news was painting them to be absolute monsters. Justin didn't feel like he was a monster. He was just determined to get it by any means necessary.

Where he grew up there weren't a lot of opportunities for advancement. That we all have the same chances line is bullshit. It's all about who you know and where you're at. Location determines what you're exposed to and what kind of knowledge you obtain. He was disgusted by the news report. Justin turned away and stormed back to the car and slammed the door.

"What was that about man?" Eddie asked bewildered by his friends seemingly erratic behavior. "I saw my face on tv and I wanted to know what they were talking bout. This shit got me not wanting to even show my face after hearing that. Cassie is definitely never coming back to me now."

"Brother you have bigger problems to worry about that a woman." Eddie retorted.

"Yeah, you right. I got the stash at your house. But I have to figure out another way to make some bread. I think they would pay for interviews or something. I'm gon look into it. You gon see my ass on Orpah talking bout this shit or something."

Eddie laughed, "I think your ass just needs to lay low. Don't be doing any tell all interviews anytime soon." They pulled up to the house. Justin went to take a shower. Eddie pulled out his computer to get back to his schoolwork. He felt bad for his friend but he couldn't be distracted. For the first time in weeks Justin's night ended peacefully.

Richard had finally stopped pacing after two hours. The 20 minutes of sleep he had managed to get the entire night had been restless. He had used his one phone call to call his wife and her number was no longer in service. It was hard for him to fathom the idea that she had been apart of this. Not his Justine who had been by his side since their youth. He had done everything to keep the business away from her. There was no way that she could have known anything.

His son had betrayed him. He loved Justin so much. It was hard for him to accept after everything that he had given him that he would just turn his back. But then again his son had changed so much since his sister's death.

Mara was the one person that understood Justin in a way nobody else in the family ever could. When she was killed a piece of his son left that day too. His anger is what made him such a fine leader in the organization. He spared nobody when it came down to getting things handled. But now in retrospect, Richard saw that turning his son into such a ruthless savage had been a mistake. There's no telling what Justin could have become, if he hadn't guided him down the wrong path.

Everything Richard held dear was gone in one night. Thinking back, he realized it had been slipping away all along. Richard didn't even know how he would pay his lawyer with his assets frozen. There was no way to access the offshore accounts from jail. Even if he did get a bond set tomorrow, who would pay it. His son and his wife were gone. For the first time since he was a little boy Richard got down on his knees and prayed. They said that prayer changes things, and he prayed with all his might for a miracle to happen to get him out of jail. But it would be in vain.

CHAPTER:VIII REDEMPTION

Iesha woke up and started making breakfast as it had become routine. She had originally said that she wouldn't do the cooking every day. Iesha changed her stance on cooking after tasting Tyrie and Cassie's cooking. Their meals made her feel like she would most surely die of food poisoning. She picked up the phone and called her Mom while the grits finishing cooking on the stove.

Loretta answered on the first ring. "Hey my beautiful baby girl how are you today?" She cheerfully asked her daughter. Donte getting Loretta out of jail had been one of the best things that had ever happened to her. Every time she heard her daughter's voice, she was so grateful.

"I'm good mama. I was just thinking about some things the other night. Being locked up in here gives you a lot of time to think."

"Chile don't I know it. You forgot I was locked down for years because of Joe's raggedy ass. Loretta said sympathetically.

"First how are my babies?" Iesha asked.

"They doing real good waiting for their pretty mama to come on home." Her mom reassured.

"I will be there as soon as I finish testifying today. These few weeks went by fast. I'm so ready to get in there and get this mess over. But mama how did you find us? I never did ask you that.

I was too excited when you first called. We have been talking about everything else."

"Well, I had a little help with locating y'all. Donte gave me enough money to do almost anything. When he got me out of jail. I used some of it to hire a private investigator after y'all went missing. Somehow he managed to find some boy that knew where y'all went." Loretta explained.

Iesha was about to ask he Mom another question, but Tyrie and Cassie came into the kitchen interrupting her conversation.

"Mama I'll call you back later. My greedy ass roomies smelled food, so they in here. They must be part bloodhound or something. I'll hit you back later on."

"Ok baby I'll be waiting." Her mom responded, then hung up.

Cassie, Iesha, and Tyrie sat down at the table. The stench of something burning hit their nostrils. "Shit the grits." Iesha hopped up and turned off the stove. Tyrie leaned over and kissed Cassie on the cheek. She looked up at him and grinned. Iesha brought the other food to the table. They passed it around and began eating.

"I'm surprised y'all two came up for air long enough to eat." Iesha said. Y'all been at it like rabbits every since the third week we was here."

Cassie looked at her best friend and rolled her eyes. "Well when you're in love that's how it be. When you find the man of your dreams, you will understand." Cassie took a bite of her eggs. Not more than two seconds after she swallowed, she ran off to the bathroom.

Iesha informed Tyrie, "That girl is pregnant. I've had enough kids. I know the signs. Y'all been using rubbers?"

Tyrie gave Iesha a mischievous grin. "I don't like swimming with no life vest." He responded.

"Well it ain't my business. But you better take care of my damn friend."

Tyrie seriously responded, "I love her and have for a long time. I'm going to spend every day showing her what real love feels like. I know she's been through a lot. I got her now. Ain't nothing or nobody going to change that."

Cassie returned to the table. "What y'all in here whispering about?" She asked them, before she gulped down some juice.

"Nothing to worry your pretty head about baby." Tyrie said, then kissed her on her forehead.

Iesha watched the two lovebirds for a moment. Then said, "We gotta hurry up. It's almost time for them to come get us for court. Y'all gotta be just as ready to get out of here as I am.

"Hell yeah. If I never see Georgia again, I won't be sorry." Cassie responded. They finished up and all got dressed. Tyrie and Cassie went to wait outside. Iesha was inside rushing trying to pack up the rest of her things.

"What are we doing after we leave here?" Tyrie asked Cassie.

She looked down at the ground a moment before she responded. "Shit I don't know but whatever it is we going to be together." She boldy stated.

Tyrie was silent a moment. Cassie thought she had made a mistake assuming they would be a couple after this was over. Finally, he spoke with a voice full of conviction. "I know you want to get out of Georgia but how about you stay with me awhile. We can figure out everything else from there."

She didn't answer but just embraced him at first. Cassie laid her head on his shoulder. It was like all the pain she had been feeling just faded away in that moment. "Yes, I'll come stay with you she answered." She thought her decision would be temporary. But she was wrong. Love is unpredictable like that. The car came and they yelled for Iesha. The threesome set out to the courthouse to finally end this nightmare and begin a new chapter of their lives.

Justin sat on Eddie's couch. He was sandwiched between his mother and his best friend. Justine had flown in the night before to support him. She had been following everything while she had been away. His mother never told him her whereabouts. The tan on her pecan-colored skin gave a clue that it was an island. Justin didn't press her for information. He felt Justine was entitled to her privacy. She at least was there, and for that he was thankful.

"Hey man you ready for this?" Eddie asked.

"Most definitely. I been crashing at your crib for far too long. I'm ready to just start over somewhere new. Mom I want you to come with me. You're all I that I have left."

"I'll think about it Justin. Lets just get through today first." His mother responded.

Justine loved her son. But she just wanted to go back into obscurity after the trial. She felt that Justin was old enough to take care of himself without her holding his hand. Besides, she had met someone. Her new man fucked her in ways Richard hadn't in years.

Eddie interrupted her thoughts, "I think we should have a farewell dinner tonight at The Spot. Y'all have been a part of my life since I can remember. I hate to see you leave. I want to send y'all off right."

Justin agreed, "That's a great idea. Now let's get out of here and get down to the courthouse.

These last few weeks in jail had really changed Richard. He was certainly humbler than before. His lawyer had brought the divorce petition earlier that morning that Justine had filed. He had signed it without any hesitation. Richard knew that life for him was over and wanted to set her free. Probably should have years ago, but he was too selfish. Justine was like a shelter in a rainstorm for him. He hoped that she could now get the love and affection that he never could quite manage for her. Him and his brother Joe had been raised on survival. Showing love wasn't something that came easy for them.

Richard now regretted letting Joe talk him into the criminal lifestyle. He only did it because at the time his family was drowning in debt. Justine never knew it. Joe saved them from being put out on the street. The money got addictive. Richard got in too deep. There was no way of getting out.

Justin killing Joe not only avenged his sister's death, but also had set his father free as well. Richard hadn't really thought about it that way previously. Being locked up and having nothing but time to think helped him realize what a true service his son had done. Richard prayed after he got his suit on for court. This time his prayers were for his ex-wife and son to move past all this pain and live normal healthy lives. He had made his peace. No matter the verdict, he had decided what he must do now.

Tangy and Donte reached the courthouse before anyone else. The flight from Morocco had been long and tiresome. But the two trudged into the courthouse hand in hand. Donte spoke first after they had made it through the metal detectors. "Are you ready to see everyone again."

"I'm still dreading seeing Unc. I thought we weren't going to have to testify. Yet here we are. I wish we could have just stayed on the islands."

Donte reassured her, "Everything is going to be ok my love. You know I'm here for you. Richard did this to himself. We are just here doing what we have to do. After this, we can move on without it hanging over our heads." He bent down and kissed his wife.

It was crazy that this mess had brought the woman of his dreams into his life. It had been love at first sight, when he met Tangy at the airport.

Being secluded on the island for weeks solidified their relationship. Donte took a chance and proposed after a swim one night. He didn't think she would accept. He was elated when she did. They had a small ceremony two weeks later on the mainland.

"Donte what the hell are you doing here!" Iesha shouting his name took his attention away from is beautiful wife. His baby cousin was in his face within in seconds with Tyrie and Cassie at her heels. The meeting in the lobby was awkward to say the least. Before, anyone in the group could utter a word in walked Justine, Justin, and Eddie. Eddie hurried on by the group and into the courtroom. He wanted no parts of that reunion. Justin and Justine approached the group timidly.

Cassie embraced Justine immediately. Tyrie feeling protective put his arm around Cassie's waist and pulled her close to him. Justin started "I just want to apologize to you all. I truly am sorry for everything I put y'all through. I know nothing I can say can justify my actions. I would like to extend an invitation to you all to join my mother and I at The Spot. We are having a dinner to celebrate new beginnings."

"This motherfucker can't be serious" Iesha angrily said.

Cassie spoke up, "I think that's a great idea." Shocking everyone. "I don't want to carry no more hate in my heart for nobody. I think this will give us all closure."

Tyrie rolled his eyes. Being around Cassie was rubbing off on him. Justin caught Tyrie's reaction, but he didn't address it.

"Well see everyone tonight at eight then." Justine and Justine then made their way inside the court room.

The group began catching up. "I'm here to testify. The FBI contacted my wife and I a few weeks ago and told us we had to come do this. Some kind of loophole in my deal.

"Wife"! Iesha and Cassie exclaimed.

Tyrie rolled his eyes again. Cassie was a little too invested in what Donte was doing for his liking.

"Yes wife. We will talk about it later. Come on. We gotta get inside. The trial is about to start." Donte told everyone. They all single file entered the courtroom and took their seats.

Richard walked inside after the group. The man looked good despite being in lock up. Justine felt a burst of emotion for her soon to be ex-husband for a split second. Just then her phone vibrated. It was a text from her new boo. He was waiting on her to get back. She didn't give her feelings for her ex a second thought. The trial passed quickly. It took all of an hour for the jury to return with a verdict of guilty.

After the sentencing everyone split up until it was time to meet later that night. Justine, Justin, and Eddie went back to his place to get all the details together for the dinner. Tyrie and Cassie went off to their hotel. Tangy, Donte, and Iesha went by Tangy's old place. There were still a few personal mementos, Tangy wanted to pick up before leaving town.

Richard was transported back to jail. Richard wrote a letter to his wife and son when he got back in his cell. Then he made a noose with his bed sheet and hung himself from the light fixture.

News of his death didn't reach the others until later that evening when they had all gathered at the restaurant.

Justine and Justin had out done themselves setting up the dinner. The place looked like it was ready for the President not a group of misfits. Everyone arrived on time and were in awe of the set up. When everyone was seated Justin went around the table and personally apologized to every single person sitting there. Replacing the generic apology from earlier at the courthouse. He then shared a secret even his best friend didn't know. His mother almost fainted. Perhaps the wine gave him liquid courage. Justin just wanted to start his new life with a clear conscious.

Right after his revelation, his mother's phone rang. When she ended the call, she informed everyone that Richard was dead. Instead of being sad, they all toasted to it. His death meant that they all were truly free to go live their lives like none of this ever happened. Justine told the prison to handle the body before she hung up. The shock of finding out her son was sleeping with his sister was still weighing heavily on her mind. She was mortified how disturbed her son really was.

The others understood his fascination with Cassie much more now. His best friend left after the news because he just didn't know what to say. They all made a pact right then and there never to mention that night again and bid each other farewell.

CHAPTER IX: ALMOST HAPPILY
EVER AFTER

Cassie had found out she was pregnant a month after the dinner hosted by Justin and his mother. She wasn't sure if the father of the baby was Tyrie or Justin. Cassie had slept with the men in close proximity to each other. When she found out she was pregnant, she didn't have the heart to tell Tyrie. They had started this new wonderful life together. Cassie didn't want the paternity of the child to put a shadow over all that. Tyrie was everything Justin had pretended to be. He was nurturing, attentive, caring, ambitious, and best of all not low-key psycho. There was no doubt their love was real.

The only snag in their relationship was his family hated her. They disliked her based on an interview she did on a talk show about her ordeal with Justin and Joe. The first time she met them didn't go well at all. Tyrie's mom had called Cassie a hoe. His grandmother had said, "I know you aren't marrying that jezebel." It was a hard pill for Cassie to swallow.

Tyrie took their words like a grain of grain of salt. He vowed he would marry her despite how they felt. The only silver lining was that his Dad thought highly of Cassie. One supporter in their corner helped out. Finally, after two months she told Tyrie the news. Neglecting to tell him he might not be the father, because she didn't want to prove his mom and grandma right.

Tyrie went to all the doctor appointments. He was such a good Daddy already. Cassie felt like an invalid because he fussed over her so much. She wasn't even big yet. Imagine how he would act when she was as big as a house with her feet all swollen.

Iesha, Tangy, and Justine had been a big support system. The trio kept in touch when they weren't visiting. Tyrie wasn't too thrilled about her still being in contact with her ex's mother. He had finally shut up about his feelings on the matter when he saw their bond.Justine was the mother that Cassie had always wished for.

Planning for a wedding and the baby kept Cassie extremely busy. She was supposed to be getting dressed to meet her fiancé for lunch instead of getting lost in her thoughts of everything that was happening around her.Her cell phone rang at that moment getting her back on track.

"Where are you? I've been here waiting like five minutes." Tyrie complained on the other end of her line."

"Im on the way. I was getting dressed and kind of spaced out. You know that has been happening to me a lot lately.

"Well get down here. My lunch break is only an hour. Cassie hurried to meet him at the little bistro around the corner.

Why didn't he come pick her up, if he was in that much of hurry? she wondered. She rushed in bumping into a familiar looking gentleman. Preoccupied with meeting Tyrie, Cassie didn't pay close enough attention.

"Finally my beautiful bride to be joins me." Tyrie said, when he laid eyes on her. He pulled out her chair and they ordered.

"Tangy and Donte are coming at the end of the week." She told him. He gave her a disgusted look. Tyrie couldn't stand the way that Donte's eyes seemed to linger on Cassie a little too long when they were in a room together.

" Don't start that shit bae. He is with Tangy. There was never anything between us."

Tyrie proclaimed, "Look I still don't trust that nigga. But for you. I'll play nice." Cassie smiled. She knew he would calm right down.

"Well I have news. I got us a wedding planner. This is too much for you to handle on your own. I don't like you being so stressed with my baby inside you."

Cassie rolled her eyes. "I told you me and Justine got it."

Tyrie stubbornly said, "Look I don't want my wedding planned by your ex's mama."

Cassie sighed she couldn't win them all. "Fine bae we can use your planner."

"Good, we are meeting her tonight when I get off work." Tyrie replied.

The food arrived. They dug in and talked less. The lunch passed by without any further disagreements. Tyrie kissed Cassie passionately before they parted ways.

Iesha called as Cassie was getting in her car to drive off. She decided to sit and chat with her friend a few minutes before heading back home.

" Hey whats up? Just calling to check on your pregnant ass." Iesha said.

"I'm good not as good as you and the billionaire." Cassie jokingly replied.

Iesha laughed, "We are not billionaires. You love to exaggerate. Every since Tyrie started his little construction company. Yall not doing so bad either."

Cassie knew something was up with her bestie. "We talking about you not me. So what's up? You never just call me in the middle of the day."

Iesha slowly responded, "Well I wanted to share my news."

Cassie impatiently asked, "What is it girl?"

"I'm pregnant" Iesha murmured.

"Damn again. Iesha don't you have nine kids?" Cassie sarcastically responded.

"Haha you so damn funny. No, its only four. Marley the baby in school now." Iesha responded.

Curiously Cassie asked, "Who is the daddy? You been all kinds of mysterious about who you have been dating since you been back home."

Iesha took a deep breath. "It's Tony."

Cassie knew it couldn't be who she thought. "Tony Tony?"

Iesha shamefully responded," Yeah girl. The nigga you wit in highschool."

Cassie angrily responded, "Iesha how could you. Bitch you know that was my first love."

Defensively Iesha responded, "Bitch youre pregnant and about to marry your dream man. How the fuck are you mad with me over a nigga you haven't seen in like five years."

Fuming Cassie responded, "It's the fucking principal Iesha. Bye, I can't deal with you right now." Cassie hung up on her friend and drove home in a rage. Who the hell gets pregnant by their best friend's first love. I cried to that girl so many times over him. I don't care if its been one year or 20. She dead ass wrong. Cassie being so upset neglected to see the car that was following her.

Tyrie got off work and they went to visit the wedding planner. Her place was beautiful. Cassie knew her and Tyrie had came up lately but she didn't think it was enough to afford all this. They sat down and Marie spoke to them to figure out what it is that they wanted. Tyrie told her he wanted to be married in a month. Cassie was shocked because they had said a year.

Tyrie pulled her off to the side. "I don't want to wait any longer. I don't want our baby being born without us being married" Tyrie explained his reason for pushing up the date.

"I didn't really take you for being the old fashioned type. Cassie replied.

"Well is it a problem?" Tyrie asked with a slight attitude. "No nigga. Now pay the lady. So we can get out of here and practice on our honeymoon." Tyrie wrote Marie a check and she assured them everything would be handled within the week. The two sauntered out into the night unknowingly being watched from the shadows.

It had been years since Frank had laid eyes on his daughter.

She had only gotten more beautiful throughout the years. He felt awful for leaving her so long ago and had tried many times to get back in contact with her. But Deloris had refused to let him see Cassie. After awhile, he just gave up. But after seeing her story on that talk show, he set out to find her again. Cassie had been through so much. Deloris couldn't cause a problem now. She was hopefully rotting in hell for what she did to his precious daughter.

He kept losing his nerve to approach his princess, after he

tracked her down. He had been following her for days now. Frank thought Cassie surely must hate him. He didn't think an apology would be enough. A simple I'm sorry wouldn't replace all the years of anguish that his presence could have prevented. Even now when she was not more the three or four feet away, he couldn't bring himself to get out of his car to talk to her. He was stuck to his seat riddled with guilt.

Contemplating a few minutes, Frank decided it was now or never and drove to his daughter's home. He arrived just as Cassie and Tyrie pulled in. He rushed out of his car and walked over to Cassie's side of the truck. His daughter took one look at his face and instantly began crying. Tyrie was reaching for his gun tucked in his waist. He always stayed strapped. Even though he went legit. His old habits didn't completely leave him.

Frank held his hands up, "Woah big fella. No need for that. I'm her dad."

Tyrie asked Cassie, "Is this true." Cassie nodded her head yes.

Frank lowered his arms. Tyrie suggested, "Well its cold out. You might as well come in to have this reunion."

Cassie immediately opened the passenger door and jumped into her father's arms. " I knew you would come back one day. I prayed and prayed. I can't believe it's finally happened," Cassie said. Sobbing on her father's shoulder. Tyrie hadn't seen his future wife display this much emotion since the day he had proposed. He made an excuse about having to make a call for work, and left Cassie and her Dad in the living room to talk.

They just sat and stared at each other for a moment. It was surreal to be in the same room together. Frank broke the silence first. "Cassie, I know this probably don't mean much to you now. I'm truly sorry for everything that has happened to you. I know if I had been there things would have been different. But that bitch wouldn't let me see you after I walked out. I don't regret leaving her. I was miserable with your money hungry mama. However, I should have fought harder to take you with me. We can't change the past. But we can make a brighter future. I would love to be a consistent part of your life. If you will let me."

Cassie sat a moment, and absorbed everything her father had just said to her. Before she responded. "Dad I would love nothing more than for us to bond like we should have been doing all along. I would like to just forget the past and just focus on the now." Frank was kind of surprised how mature Cassie sounded for being only 23 years old. "Well, I'm not sure how much you know. Seeing as you have been snooping around. But, you have a grandchild on the way.

Maybe you can show him or her the things that you didn't get a chance to do with me."

"I would love that. It's getting late baby girl. Here's my number. Call me tomorrow. We can meet and catch up more. I don't want to over stay my welcome. Your boyfriend didn't look too thrilled about me just popping up here."

"I'll handle him. I'll definitely call you tomorrrow Dad. The two hugged and Cassie walked her father out.

Tyrie reappeared immediately after Cassie reentered the living room. "That was a really long call bae."

Tyrie laughed. I didn't want to get in the middle of your family reunion. I do have more sense than you give me credit for."

"Hush man and come give me some loving." Tyrie obliged and kissed his lady on the lips.

"Mrs. Davis are you ready for bed ma'am." "Mmhmmm I'm tired as fuck. My daughter is ready for bed too."

" You mean my son. Obviously it's a boy."

"Hmph you think that. I know what I know and it's a girl."

Tyrie swatted her bottom. "What I say."

Cassie looked over her shoulder and rolled her eyes. "Im not about to play wit you. That's how we got in this predicament in the first place."

Tyrie laughed. "After you drop that one. You will be in a predicament again."

Cassie finished taking off her clothes and got under the covers. "You are not about to keep me bare foot and pregnant."

Tyrie rubbed her stomach. "Just hold on lil guy. We going to have you five or six siblings to play with."

Cassie rolled her eyes again. Even though it was dark and Tyrie couldn't see her. "Hush you tired. Take your ass to sleep." Cassie turned over and instantly knocked out.

Tyrie crawled in bed beside her and wrapped his arms around her. All was right in their little world for just a moment.

The weeks until the wedding flew by without incident. The planner was a miracle worker and got everything set up in the time limit that Tyrie had requested. Tyrie's family even came around. Well, everyone except his grandmother. She was insistent on the fact you can't turn no hoe into a housewife.

Cassie and her father had gotten close. It was like he had never left her side at all. Finally, the love that Cassie had been craving all these years she was getting from her father and Tyrie. Letting go of Iesha had been hard. But this was the second time she had crossed Cassie. She decided that she wouldn't give her a chance for a third. Besides her friendships with Tangy and Justine were authentic. She knew that both of them truly had her back without ulterior motives.

They wedding was small and intimate. Everything was immaculately decorated. It was more than the couple had hoped for. Justine and tangy were Cassie's bridesmaids. Her father walked her down the aisle. When the preacher asked if anyone objected to the union, Justin burst through the doors and nearly gave Cassie a heart attack.

But he just sat in the back of the church and didn't interrupt the ceremony. Justine turned red because she was so upset.

As soon as the wedding was over, Justine pulled her son outside. "What the hell are you doing here." I thought you were still getting treatment at the clinic."

"Mom I'm better. I feel better than I ever have. I know I shouldn't have come. I just needed to get closure. Real closure. I really did love Cassie. I just wanted to make sure all this was real before I finally let go."

"Boy get the hell out of here. Let that girl enjoy her day. She has been through too much. I have taught you way better than this."

"Mama I'm gone after I leave here. I got a good job overseas.

Daddy's connections are still some good."

"Don't go getting yourself into some bullshit Justin. I just don't have the heart for it."

Chauncey walked up to the pair and kissed Justine on the cheek. "Baby is everything ok?" He said. Eyeing Justin. Chauncey saw the similarities but him and the kid looked only a few years apart. Justine couldn't possibly be old enough to have a son that old. He never thought to ask her how old she was.

"He is just leaving sweetie don't worry yourself."

Justin looked kind of shocked, but he bid his mother farewell and left. "He couldn't believe how cold she had been to him. But he guessed he deserved it. Carrying on like he had been any mother would have had enough. He hoped that one day that him and his mother could reconcile but he was truly happy that Cassie had found normalcy finally.

In a way it was like the gift that he could never give his sister. Eddie was waiting for Justin in the parking lot of the venue. He was taking Justin to the airport. Justin hadn't told him where he was going. Eddie just knew that his friend was going away to start a new life. He felt that was the best for everyone.

Even though he knew Justin was messed up he couldn't turn his back on him. They had been friends for far too long. They were really all each other had at this point. Eddie's dad was never getting out of jail. What members of his family didn't get locked up were in hiding somewhere because of all the firm business. When they got to the airport, Eddie gave his friend a big hug and handed him a small envelope. He knew that Justin still hadn't built himself back up yet. He hoped that the money would help his friend's fresh start be better.

Meanwhile back at the wedding, Chauncey and Justine re-entered the reception. Cassie was glowing, looking like she had forgotten that her psycho ex had crashed the wedding. Her and Tyrie were on the dancefloor showing out.

Tangy grabbed Justine by the arm as she walked back in and pulled her off to the side. Chauncey walked off to talk to Donte since he didn't know anyone else there. They had met a couple of times recently at Cassie's place.

"Is everthing alright?" I know my cousin and he isn't really the giving up type."

"Yes, everything is fine love go enjoy the party. After the exchange Justine joined everyone else on the dance floor. Just because she was older didn't mean she still didn't have her moves. Cassie gave her a worried look and Justine gave her the thumbs up. Cassie breathed a sigh of relief. The party continued well into the late evening. Tyrie took his tired bride home they would leave for the honeymoon in the morning Well so they thought.

The next morning Cassie awoke before her husband and went to make him breakfast. while she was cooking, her phone started ringing uncontrollable. Who the hell could this be at this hour she wondered. "Hello, Im calling from the hospital. A Frank Lewingston has you down as next of kin."

"Yes that's my father. Whats going on?"

"Your father was brought in this morning. He was complaining of severe chest pains. He has coded twice. We really need you to come down here immediately. Cassie turned off the stove and rushed out of the house. She couldn't lose her daddy twice.

She arrived at the hospital in record speed. She ran up to the front desk asking them which room her father was in. They told her and she took the stairs, too impatient to wait for the elevator. When she reached his room, the doctor was just coming out. She hurriedly ran over to him. He asked her was she a relative.

"Yes I'm his daughter. How is my dad?"

"Your Dad was touch and go for awhile, but he will be fine. You can go in to see him if you like."

She rushed in to see her father. His eyes opened as soon as she walked into the room. Cassie just sat on the edge of the bed and held his hand. "I thought I was losing you again."

"I'm a tough old bird. it will take more than a few chest pains to take me out," Frank said.

"I'm just glad you're still here dad. I want you to come stay with us for a few days."

"I don't want to impose honey."

"No I insist. Let me take care of you Dad."

"Aren't you supposed to be off on your honeymoon."

"Yeah but that can wait. Im going to tell Tyrie as soon as I get back home."

" Well I think that should be soon. Can't have any daughter of mine parading around town in pajamas.

Cassie looked down at her clothes for the first time, realizing she was still in pjs. "I forgot all about that. I was just trying to get here."

"I appreciate it. I'll be fine."

"Ok Dad. im going to change and talk to Tyrie. I'll be back."

"I'll be right here waiting." Cassie kissed her father on the cheek. Then headed home to face her husband.

When she reached the house it was eerily quiet. She found Tyrie outside smoking a blunt. He must have found her stash, because he usually didn't smoke anything but cigarettes. She crept up behind him and he jumped when she touched his arm. "Girl dont do that shit. You scared me half to death. Where have u been? I called your phone about 50 times."

"I was at the hospital. Dad had a heart attack. I just rushed out after I got the call."

" I see that. Youre still in your night clothes."

" I was just so scared Tyrie. I cant lose him. He is all I have left."

"Well you got me and our baby now too."

"You know what I mean. I want Dad to stay at the house a few days. Just to make sure he is really ok."

"That's fine baby. I understand how much he means to you. We can put everything else off for now." She hugged her husband. He kissed her forehead and didn't say anything for awhile. Eventually they both got dressed and went back to the hospital to check on Frank.

Frank came home with them the next day. Cassie dauted on him even though he insisted that she didn't need to do that. Their bond got even deeper. Whether he admitted or not, he had been lonely. Being in his daughter's company was more of a blessing than she knew. When her and Tyrie finally decided to go on their honeymoon a few months later, he was in his own place a few blocks away. He had decided that he would put down roots near his daughter. He wanted to be in her and his granchild's life daily if possible.

The weeks after the honeymoon went by in a blur. Eventually the newlyweds had a baby shower. Justine and Tangy came to town to help with the shower. The two ladies wouldn't let Cassie do anything. She was big enough to pop. Later that night she did. She had a beautiful baby girl that she named Destiny. Cassie felt that everything she had been through was for that moment. When the nurse handed her the baby and she looked at her face for the first time, all she could think of was how much her eyes looked just like Justin's.

Sneak Peek:
Jezebel Part Two (Saving Destiny)

"Mmm. Yes Daddy! This dick feels so good!" I screamed. "Take that shit like a pro Destiny. I know you can throw that ass back better than that." Kai said, cheering me on while he sat in his computer chair watching me fuck his home boy. The whole room filled up with the scent of loud suddenly. Kai must have finished rolling the blunt and lit it.

Kai walked over to the bed where I was still getting my pussy pounded by Bryant. While puffing on the blunt he pulled my head up by gripping a handful of my hair. "Open your mouth Des." He demanded. I eagerly obliged and Kai blew me a shotgun. All the smoke from the blunt filled my mouth and lungs.

Before I could exhale the smoke completely Kai had filled my mouth with his thick 10-inch dick. Meanwhile Bryant was still hitting me from the back. He was deep in my guts. The only sounds in the room were my slurping and Bryant's balls slapping against my ass with each thrust of his 10.5 inch dick into my soaking wet pussy.

Kai passed the blunt to Bryant so he could have both his hands free to fuck my face. Bryant grabbed the blunt without getting out of sync with his stroke. You could see the imprint of Kai's dick perfectly as he slammed it deeper and deeper down my throat.

I had learned to breath through just my nose a long time ago. So coming up for air wasn't even a issue. The faster Kai fucked my throat the more I nutted on Bryant's dick. Bryant finally bust his nut.

He threw the condom in the trash beside the dresser. Passed the blunt to Kai who had just pulled out my mouth so he could bust his nut all over my face.

Bryant was done since that was his third nut of the night. He poured a shot of Henny from the bottle that was sitting on the desk. Threw his boxers back on and took the spot Kai had previously been seated in. Kai took over where Bryant left off behind me. Kai loved to tease. He stuck his index finger in my ass and his middle one in my pussy. "Damn girl you gushy." Kai murmured. Bryant agreed, "Yeah we got ourselves a winner. This time. Bro." Kai passed the blunt back to Bryant.

Then he started sliding his fully erect large dick in my ass. It hurt like hell but I just buried my face in the pillow. No way was I showing weakness in front of Bryant. Kai knew I was too damn stubborn to tap out in front of an audience. That is why he picked this particular moment to do anal.

Bryant fell into a drunk sleep in the chair before Kai finished punishing my ass. "Damn Kai that's enough. We been at this anal shit for like 20 minutes." I whined. "Girl if you don't shut up. I'm almost done." He responded. True to his word two mins later his nut was running out my ass and down my thigh. Mixing with my own that was already there.

I stood up after he was done. Kai pulled me close and tongue kissed me, "I love you Destiny," He said looking at me all serious." I know." I said. He rolled his eyes. "I love you too bae. Now roll up while I take a shower. Wake Bryant up and tell him to get out of our room.

I'm going to take a bath, Bring me the blunt when you get it ready." Kai rolled his eyes again.

" You think I'm Alfred or Jeffrey don't you. He said making reference to batman's butler and the one on this show called the Fresh Prince. "Boy just do what I said." I walked away and into our master bathroom. Started preparing my bath water in our corner bathtub. I had to pour my essential oils in to keep my caramel skin smooth. I added in some epson salt and sea salt too. I definitely needed to soak my soreness and cleanse after that episode we just had in our bedroom. The whirlpool jets would help elevate my soreness as well.

I heard Kai waking Bryant up. Bryant was knocking stuff over, he was so intoxicated, The bedroom door closed just as the tub was at the perfect water level for me to get in. I slid down in the tub until the water covered my shoulders. This soak felt so good after Bryant and Kai had me folded up like a pretzel half the night.

I was drifting off to sleep in the tub when Kai bust in interrupting my peace talking all loud. "Here girl take this blunt." He said as he handed it to me. Along with a glass of Henny on ice. "Thanks bae. I said and he sat down on the edge of the tub and kissed my lips.

"Destiny do you ever miss the you before all this he asked." " I said, " Naw because then I wasn't free. I was just going through life pretending. That other Destiny well she wasn't really me." I responded. I took a swallow of my drink. Handed Kai my washcloth and he started washing my back. I took a long pull off the blunt. "Bae, I still can't believe you let me fuck your best friend." I said to Kai. "Well I know you gon be you. Plus he going back home next week anyway. So what does it matter. It's not like you don't let me fuck other bitches so what's the difference." Kai stated. "That's cause I know you too. I looked at him and laughed. "Girl finish washing your ass so we can go to bed. I'm tired. Its been a long ass night, Kai said.

"Bae go change the sheets I'm not sleeping in y'all nigga's nut tonight. " I insisted. Kai took his tall yellow skinny behind in the room to do like I asked. I kept relaxing with my blunt and drink, I know you wondering how I ended up with my man and his best friend. But, hell I was Bryant's woman first.